The Bonds of Death

The Bonds of Death

Published by The Nazca Plains Corporation
Las Vegas, Nevada
2006

ISBN: 1-887895-21-3

Published by

The Nazca Plains Corporation ®
4640 Paradise Rd, Suite 141
Las Vegas NV 89109-8000

PUBLISHER'S NOTE
The Bonds of Death is a work of fiction created wholly by
the author's imagination. All characters are fictional and any
resemblance to any persons living or deceased is purely by
accident. No portion of this book reflects any real person or
events.

Cover Art by Ross Johnston
Editor, Blake Stephens

Dedication

To Michael, who inspired all that is good in my life.

Acknowledgments

There are so many people to thank when a novel finally becomes published. First, I would like to thank Michael Rowe. A busy author, he spent a great deal of time encouraging me to write and to pursue publication for the stories. Then, of course, a special thanks to Tim Brough who kindly read my work and passed it along to be considered by his publisher. To my partner/spouse/lover/slave, Michael who provided inspiration and support through this whole process. And finally, to a man named John who I used to call 'Sir'. The lessons he taught me about leather, life, and love will always direct my life.

The Bonds of Death

Chuck Williams

Contents

Chapter 1

As Colin Morgan stepped out of the coffee shop in Squirrel Hill, a refreshing, almost cold, breeze surprised him. It was unseasonably cool for late August in Pittsburgh, and, while the rest of humanity dreaded this as a sign of summer's end, Colin welcomed it. He absolutely hated the summer heat. His lover, Derek, was just the opposite; he loved the summer and hated the cold of the winter. Of course, they were opposites in so many respects, which made the relationship interesting, and, at times, tense.

The Squirrel Hill section of Pittsburgh was such a picturesque community. It was made up of Russian Jewish immigrants, university students, and various types of yuppies. At any given moment, you could encounter a Hasidic Jew, young people with pierced eyes, ears, and noses with green hair, or a *bona fide* Eddie Bauer wearing, Cherokee driving yuppie. Being so close to Pittsburgh's many universities and colleges, Squirrel Hill exuded an air of tolerance. It's ever growing business area was surrounded by some of the most beautiful houses and most expensive real estate in the city. Colin loved the subdued energy of its streets and coffee shops.

Walking down a tree-lined street to the car, Colin experienced a slight pang of guilt. Not more than two hours ago, he had the most incredible sex with Billy. Billy was a man who managed to have an effect on Colin, and there weren't many men who could claim that accomplishment. He was twenty-three years old, with a great body, and a face that could only be described as beautiful. Billy stood about five feet nine inches tall and had a wiry, muscular physique. His blond hair framed his deep blue eyes. Eyes that seemed to pierce right through you. When he smiled, his whole face lit up, creating an almost infectious good mood for anyone coming into contact with it. Furthermore, he maintained that boyish quality of appearing to have no direction in his life, spending his time in a low paying, dead-end job. It was interesting how that could be so attractive to a slightly older man.

Colin couldn't resist Billy, especially when the younger man called with that special tremor in his voice indicating that he needed sex. Not just sex, but rough, intense sex.

When he had called earlier that day, Colin managed to finish quickly at the hospital and raced over to his apartment. They both dispensed with the preliminary cordialities that most friends share when they meet. Billy, almost instantly, had been forced to his knees, licking Colin's shoes and pants and finally resting his open mouth on Colin's still unzipped crotch. Before long, Billy was tied up, with Colin administering the various torments that they, along with all other leather men, found thrilling: hot wax, clamps, and little whipping. Finally, Colin untied him, bent him over, and fucked him roughly. The scene ended with the now unfettered boy kneeling again at his feet while Colin bathed him with a stream of hot piss.

After they had cleaned up, Colin and Billy sat entwined on the couch, each savoring the afterglow of satisfaction that usually follows a very fulfilling sexual experience. Colin had no compunction about meeting Billy from time to time. He, Derek, and Billy often had found themselves in bed together after a three-way that was remarkably similar to the just ended scenario. Besides, Derek had been ignoring him quite a bit these days. And while there are times when a lover would stray to punish their partner, that wasn't the case between Billy and Colin. Colin truly loved Derek and looked at the past couple of hours as simply lightening Derek's load, not to mention the lightening of his load onto Billy. If he and Derek had never played together with Billy at one time, he wouldn't have been in the young man's apartment this afternoon.

He pulled the Grand Cherokee into the garage and was surprised to find that Derek was already home. It wasn't even ten o'clock yet, and his lover had been coming home well after that for the past few weeks. It was even more of surprise when Colin discovered Derek asleep in their bed, and not working at his desk. As he watched his lover at rest, Colin realized that nothing could ever really come between him and Derek. He quickly undressed, and slipping in beside him, nestled the man in his arms.

Before either one of them could realize what was happening, Colin's hard-on had caused Derek to stir, and, for the second time that night for him, and the first time for Derek, they made love. Their lovemaking contrasted sharply with the intense S/M experience that Colin just had with Billy. It was tender, perhaps even sublime. Both came quickly and Colin let his dick rest inside Derek for a few minutes before pulling out, each of them savoring the union of their bodies. After it was over, he was quite proud of himself, thinking, "Not bad for a thirty-eight year old hospital administrator." Of course, he had always been proud of his sexual prowess, which was the talk among many of his set. However, before he could dwell any longer on these thoughts, he and Derek fell into the kind of deep sleep that lovers often experience when the emotions of their hearts are validated by the passion of their bodies.

They really hadn't been together all that long. Colin often forgot that it had been only five years. In many ways they seemed to have been together from birth. Had anyone suggested that he would be in love with, and married to, an Episcopal priest, he would simply have laughed. It just wasn't his style. Fuck them, yes. Torture them, yes. Have dinner with them, yes. Fall in love? No. Marry them? Never. But, as life often teaches us, Colin learned that using the word never was a challenge to the powers-that-be to make some changes in his life.

Although he had an advanced degree in philosophy, it was his training as a microbiologist, and later as a hospital administrator, that tended to define him. Colin, a relatively hot man in his late-thirties, was known throughout his profession as a gifted administrator, and among his peers in the leather world as a very proficient Master. The idea that he would also be the spouse of an Episcopal rector just didn't fit in with those definitions. Yet, when he met Derek, he couldn't resist him.

At first, it was not easy for either of them. Colin met his lover in a bar when he was out of town at a conference. They were just gong to have a one-night stand. But quite a one-night stand it was. The sex had been hot and intense, with Derek amazed that this man could take him to the very edge of his limits in sadomasochism. After that, they stayed up all night talking about every subject that could be thought of, and before dawn, each had fallen in love with the other.

The next morning, in the naked light of day, they realized that they lived about four hundred miles apart. It was then that the reality of the night before set in. After what could only be called a tumultu-ous courtship, they finally agreed that Derek would come and try it in Pittsburgh. Luckily enough, he was called to be the rector of a very progressive church, smack dab in the middle of a very conservative and reactionary diocese. Each day he was faced with the challenge of a bishop who would have loved to get rid of him as a priest in his diocese. A priest, who, in the bishop's mind, was an abomination before the Lord. But the church was wealthy and influential, and the bishop wanted to avoid making the parishioners unhappy. Therefore, Fr. Derek stayed on in the little High Church parish, ministering to his flock with the assistance of a curate, the Rev. Millicent Barclay.

For his part, Colin realized that Derek was unhappy, and was willing to follow his lover's career, where ever that would lead. However, since Colin had an exponentially higher salary than Derek, economics had won the day. Every morning, Colin still reviewed the job lists for his profession, looking for a place where he and his lover could live without anxiety. Their place of residence was often the starting point in an argument, and Colin realized that something had to be done soon. They had entered into a truce in the war about the subject. But it was an uneasy truce with continued minor skirmishes from time to time.

It wasn't that Pittsburgh was all that bad. It was actually a beautiful place with hills and rivers and wonderful housing stock. Granted, it was still trying to find its economic foothold after the collapse of the steel industry, but it was trying. It boasted a world class symphony, a resident ballet and opera company, and some of the most fascinating art galleries and museums in the country. Derek had problems with the city mainly because he was a gay Episcopal priest. Pittsburgh tended to be a little conservative, at least on the surface, and gay life was not as varied or as visible as it was in other cities. In many ways, it was a city with a small town mentality.

While they did love each other, that's not to say that there were no arguments. Colin was jealous that so much time was taken up with Derek's responsibilities. He had forgotten what it was like in the early years of a profession, any profession. He had worked for over ten years as an administrator, and the work came easily to him. A young Rector of a parish didn't have the same kind of professional ease. Of course, Millicent didn't help the situation either. She was needy. Having been in a bad marriage for some time, she turned to Derek for support. Derek, who was always more comfortable in the company of women, found a friend, a colleague, and a confidant. Colin tried to be open and understanding, but most of the time he looked at it as more of an intrusion. Not that Derek couldn't have a friend, but Millicent had a strong personality, and a great deal of influence over Derek. Colin had seen it time and time again, a straight woman, unhappy with her situation in life, attaches to a gay man, and forms an almost marriage like bond of friendship. When Millicent had issues, Derek had issues. When Millicent was excited about something, Derek became excited about it. While this wasn't necessarily bad, what was distressing was that when Millicent was unhappy with her spouse, Derek often became hypercritical of his.

Millicent and Colin were certainly friendly with one another. It was, however, a friendship born out of situation and not desire. If Derek were to have any peace in his life, these two people simply had to get along. And get along they did, much the same way that two strong willed animals got along in the same forest. A friendship formed on the intimidation of the power that each held over the common thread, Derek. Millicent couldn't understand the dynamic of dominance and submission in a gay S/M relationship. She challenged both Colin and Derek about it. Colin, used to his sexual partners doing exactly what they were told, was uneasy when the man kneeling before him at night was also the man discussing their finances the next day. And everyone knows that S/M Masters have one need that must always be tended to: their egos – they need to feel like they are in charge, even when they aren't. And Derek was confused about his role as spiritual leader of a church, friend to his colleagues, and sexual slave to a man that he not only loved, but admired as well. It was the respect that each of them had for the other that kept them together when their love was obscured by the intensity of their personalities.

They lived in a parish house, or rectory, which was brought over stone by stone from England at the beginning of the century. The rectory was a large building that was built to resemble a small English cottage. It was made entirely of stone with fireplaces in every room. While updated electricity and plumbing had been added, central heat and air conditioning had not. This only seemed to validate Derek's dislike of winter. After Derek got the position at St. Swithen's, Colin sold his condominium and moved in with his lover, becoming, in many ways, the Rector's wife, a role that was not usually a part of the repertoire of a leather top. The congregation was supportive, but Colin could never determine whether they were truly supportive or just liked the idea of having a gay priest and his spouse in the parish, as if their acceptance of them was a totem of liberalism. He got along with just about every one in the parish, except the gay men. To him they were effeminate, and, at best dysfunctional. Derek was kinder in his assessment of people. He would often give his lover a supportive glance across a room when he noticed Colin's smile, cemented on his face as he endured yet another discussion on the nature of altar linens from some man who felt it was his life's work to be a member of the Altar Guild. It was that cemented smile, and that supportive glance that affirmed and strengthened their love for one another.

However, when it came to the bishop, Colin was much more understanding than his lover was. The Right Reverend Barnabus Walsingham was a force to be reckoned with. At this time, Pittsburgh didn't have a residential Episcopal bishop. There had been warring factions over who would be right for the job. In the end, an interim bishop took over the reins of power until the conflict could be resolved. Standing only five feet three inches in height, Bishop Walsingham often wore a mitre that was so tall, it looked as if a hobbit had suddenly donned the vestments of a bishop and appeared before the congregation. Derek railed against the man, saying that he was the downfall of the Episcopal Church, while Colin simply referred to him as Bishop Bilbo, and looked on him as a comic figure, having no real power. Colin, ever true to his S/M lifestyle liked being in the bishop's presence, he liked making him uncomfortable. And with the razor sharp wit that was a characteristic of gay men from the seventies, he often managed to have entire conversations with the man who had no understanding of what was being said to or about him. The bishop, zealous as he was, he was not known for his intellect. It was regarding this man that Derek and Millicent had their one and only disagreement – she liked him. In many ways, she could overlook his stand on gay rights and other social issues, saying that in other ways he was a good man. Derek stood his ground. And Colin, who, at times could be rather mean spirited, once asked Millicent if the good bishop were as opposed to women's ordination as to the ordination of gay men, would she be as understanding. Always the peacemaker, Derek asked that they no longer discuss the bishop in the presence of his lover.

Chapter 2

When the radio came on in the morning, Colin turned over to embrace his lover, and found only a cold pillow. As he was slowly trying to understand this, he heard Derek's voice from the kitchen, "Come on, hurry up, I made breakfast, and if you get down here quickly enough, we can have a meal just like the straight people do every morning."

As he pulled himself out of bed, he wondered how in the world he had managed to settle down with a morning person. It was just unnatural for a gay man to get up at the crack of dawn. "OK, give me a couple of minutes," he called down.

When he got to the kitchen, he was amazed. Derek had really made breakfast: pancakes, sausages, toast, and eggs. It was an unusually elaborate breakfast for the two men, they simply didn't eat this much most mornings.

"What's on your agenda today?" Colin asked as he sat down.

"Let's see – I have a couple of meetings this morning, a funeral at two, and a dinner downtown."

"Who died?"

"Oh, no one from the parish, it was somebody originally from here who wished to be brought back to be buried. Actually, he was a rather young man, only thirty."

"AIDS?"

"No, not this time, some kind of cancer. I actually feel a little uncomfortable doing the funeral, I didn't know him, and that's always a disadvantage."

"Remember, we're supposed to meet Dirk for drinks a little later this evening," Colin reminded his ever-forgetful lover.

"I know, I have it in my book, and I am going to make it," Derek answered with a smirk on his face that indicated that he knew that his lover thought that he had forgotten.

"That's amazing. Of course, do we really want to spend time with him? I know that he's our friend, but since he has become Mr.

Steel City Leather, he has become almost unbearable."

"Come on Colin, he's not that bad. We *do* like him, even if he isn't that bright. And we haven't been with too many gay men lately, at least ones that aren't interested in the anthem sung on Sundays or the Belgian lace they found for the Mary Chapel. . .but I don't ever want to have sex with him"

"That's true, but if he wears that sash, I'm going to let him have it."

"Just let it drop Colin, it's not really that bad."

After that, Colin cleaned up the kitchen and got ready for work. He stopped in his lover's office before leaving and kissed the man lightly on the cheek.

"You're being exceptionally tender these days. What gives? Don't you like tying me up any more?"

"There simply hasn't been time lately, and a man has needs."

"Well, we're going out tonight, and I have nothing all day tomorrow."

"A Saturday without a wedding or some practice?"

"Yes, and you and I can spend all night fooling around, and all day tomorrow doing whatever you want."

"OK, but when we meet tonight trade that linen collar in for my leather one."

"You got yourself a deal, Sir," Derek replied.

With that, they said good-bye and Colin made his way to the hospital and his office. He always got to the office early, this morning was the exception, and of course, there was a line of people waiting to see him. He hated that. While he detested getting up early in the morning, it was worth it to have a few minutes peace before the world came crashing down on him, and in a hospital, that happened all the time. He was amazed that people who were proficient and well educated thought that every little thing was a major crisis. He didn't care if a nurse had been ten minutes late four times in the past six months, he didn't see the necessity of suspending or firing him. Yet, hospital supervisors could often be so meticulous about these things. Educated they may be, but intelligent they definitely were not, at least not in Colin's critical eyes.

Martin, his very efficient assistant, came in when the crowds disappeared. "You have a lunch meeting today with the Ukrainian visiting surgical fellow."

"Who is this, and why am I having lunch with him?"

"He requested it."

"But he doesn't even know me."

"All the same, I've made reservations for you at a restaurant on the South Side."

Colin couldn't imagine that a surgeon requested to have lunch, or even meet with him. They tended only to stay with their own kind, other surgeons. At best, hospital administrators were the enemy, at least, most of the time. When they needed a new surgical suite or some new and expensive technology, they would often come, hat in hand, acting like administrators were part of the team, but the rest of the time they simply looked upon them as a necessary evil.

"What's his name?"

"Vladimir Vostik."

"OK, is he meeting me there or here?"

"You're supposed to pick him up at his home."

"That's ridiculous! Call him and tell him to meet me in my office!"

"Colin, you can't alienate him, he's some brilliant surgeon, and it's a major coupe that we have him here," his assistant admonished.

"All the same, tell him to meet me here. Tell him that hospital needs require it."

"OK, but I think you are making a mistake."

After Martin left, Colin tackled the ever-present stack of papers on his desk. He was still fuming over the fact that some hotshot surgeon wanted him to act like his personal servant. The morning went by quickly and surprisingly without many interruptions. As it turned out, he actually had the time to go and meet the man at his home. Nevertheless, he had made a stand based on principle, and that was always important to Colin.

When Martin knocked on the door and opened it with Dr. Vostik in tow, Colin was sorry that he hadn't gone to the man's home. Standing before him was perhaps the hottest man that he had ever seen.

Vladamir stood five feet eleven inches in height and weighed about 180. He had broad shoulders which tapered to a perfect 'V' at his waist. Coal black hair and deep blue eyes adorned a face that was flawless. Everything about him seemed like perfection to Colin.

"Hello Mr. Morgan, I'm very glad to meet you," he said in

accented English.

"Please call me Colin, Dr. Vostik. The pleasure is all mine."

"Then you must call me Vlad, Colin."

"Fine Vlad, and I hope that you will accept my apology for not coming by to pick you up this morning. There was quite a bit of work waiting for me. Fridays are always the worst days here."

"No problem, I'm glad that we can have lunch this afternoon. And I promise not to keep you too long. But you must drive. I haven't a clue how anyone can find their way around Pittsburgh."

Martin stepped in to intercede. He saw the look on Colin's face and simply knew that his boss wouldn't mind wasting an afternoon over coffee and drinks with this handsome man. "Oh, Mr. Morgan, don't worry about hurrying back. I've cleared your calendar for the afternoon. I thought that you would perhaps like a jump on the weekend," Martin interjected, knowing that his boss wanted to jump on the young Ukrainian hunk standing in front of them.

"Thank you Martin, and please, you don't have to revert to the Mr. Morgan just because we have company. That's not my style."

The handsome Ukrainian surgeon and the administrator walked down the hall and out of the building. The drive to the restaurant was filled with small talk. Where did you go to medical school? What is the former Soviet Union like now? What's the hospital like? What is there to do in Pittsburgh? It turned out that Vlad was only three years younger than Colin, but he looked about twenty five. They crossed one of the three rivers that Pittsburgh was known for, and soon were seated in a quiet, dark Spanish restaurant.

"I have a confession to make, Colin."

"Yes?"

"I have been in Pittsburgh for about a week now. I stopped into the *Pirate's Nest* last week and asked what was hot in Pittsburgh. They told me you, and I thought that perhaps I could lure you into a little play today at the house that I am renting."

"Well, you have managed to find your way around Pittsburgh a little bit. Unfortunately the *Pirate's Nest* isn't a great leather bar, but it's all that we have. Pittsburgh hasn't had its gay revolution yet. We're still waiting for it."

"But it's so beautiful here. Why aren't there more gay people?"

"Actually there are a lot, and quite a bit about the non-visible gay community has to do with all of the ethnic groups that have settled here and maintained their traditions and communities once there were settled. The Germans, and the Ruthenians, the Carpatho-Russyns, and a whole bunch of others maintained their own cultures once they settled here. There was a great deal of acceptance because each group had their own prejudices directed against each other. Gay people became just another ethnic minority, and we are expected to maintain our culture within our community and on our religious feast days."

"Gay people have religious feast days in this country?" A perplexed Vlad asked.

"Halloween, Judy Garland's birthday, and the anniversary of the Stonewall riots."

The two men dissolved into laughter as they both admired the particularly attractive rear end on the Spanish waiter as he cleared the table. The two pitchers of Sangria that they shared at lunch intensified the laughter. As they waited for coffee, Vlad posed the inevitable question, "So, are we going to play together?"

Colin stared directly into his eyes and smiled a little as he answered, "You know that I have a lover."

"Yes, and I've been told that you often play with a third."

"You seem to have been told quite a bit in your short stay in Pittsburgh. Apparently, I have a fan club. Don't anticipate too much, you could be disappointed."

"Not by what I see in front of me. Is it true that you've slept with some pretty famous people?"

"Yes, and I'm not about to name names. The people who knew who I slept with in my younger years are, unfortunately, dead. So the secret remains safe with me."

"But your famous partners, are they dead as well?"

"A couple, but most of them are very much alive. I hope that you don't mind, but let's change the subject. I have always maintained that reliving your sexual past was only appropriate when a man reaches the down hill side of his life. I hope that I haven't reached that stage yet."

"No, not from what I can see."

"Look, it's Friday night and my lover isn't busy at all tomorrow. We are meeting friends at that awful leather bar that you have already found. Join us for a drink. We can discuss sexual matters there."

"What does your lover do?"

"He's a priest." Colin loved saying it just like that and leaving it for the entire world to comprehend. Having been raised a Catholic himself, although he became an Episcopalian after meeting Derek, he knew the taboo associated with despoiling a priest.

"And he's open about it?" Was the only reply that Vlad could possibly make.

"Actually he's an Episcopal priest. They are a little more forgiving than the Catholic or Orthodox are on the matter. Although, since their central authority mechanisms are not that strong, individual bishops can often promote their own biased agenda."

"Is he as hot as you are?"

"Yes, and he's a lot prettier than I am. He has that blond English choirboy look that drives me crazy. And he's younger than I am, only twenty-nine."

"How long have you two been together?"

"A little over five years."

"He wasn't much more than a choirboy when you met him then."

"Oh yes he was. Newly ordained, but he had been around the block a few times before I took the reins."

As they finished their coffee, they talked about all sorts of things. Much more meaningful things than the playful small talk they shared when they first met. Colin was taking his time, trying to sober up, before attempting to get in the car and drive through the small crooked streets that surrounded Pittsburgh. They had spent the better part of the afternoon having conversations ranging from the philosophy and impact of managed care to gay life in the Ukraine. Vlad was a wonderful man. Colin knew that they would couple sexually in the near future, and since Vlad was here for at least three years, it might be a scene that could be played over repeatedly.

"Well Dr. Vostik, where do you live? I couldn't come and pick you up, but I certainly will take you home. Or, did you park at the hospital?"

"No, I took the bus to the hospital. I told you I couldn't figure out these streets. I live in Shadyside. I thought that was where all the boys lived."

"Yes it is. I live in Friendship. It's the neighboring section of town to Shadyside. . . and that's where all the men live."

"And your lover's church, where is it?"

"Right beside the house. I am the Rector's husband."

"And does that mean that they call you the Rectorina?" He asked laughing.

"You can bring that up to Derek."

"What do I call him? Derek? Father? Reverend?"

"Depending on your station in the leather community, you could call him BOY. But Derek will do for now."

They got into the car and Vlad was impressed at how short a distance it really was to his house. When you know the roads, one area of Pittsburgh was not all that far from the other, inside the city limits. As Colin drove up to the address that Vlad had given him he realized that he knew the house. It belonged to a gay couple, old friends of his and new friends of Derek.

"Are you living with Michael and Lee?"

"No, Michael and Lee have rented me the house for the time that I am going to be here."

"Where are they living?"

"Lee has taken a visiting professor position in Philadelphia and Michael has gone along to be a housewife and write the great American gay novel. Or, at least, that's what I was told."

"It's a great house, you'll love it." Colin couldn't help but remembering when his friend Lee Starr bought the house. Lee was great, and, if Colin hadn't found Derek they might have been together today. Lee was an accomplished English professor at a local university. All the same, he was a little flighty. When he went to the closing on this house, all of the papers read Ms. Lee Starr, single female. Needless to say, Lee would never live that one down. As a matter of fact, Derek and Colin's Christmas card was always addressed: Ms. Lee Starr, Single Female.

"How about I pick you up around ten tonight, and you come to the bar with us?" Colin asked as Vlad was getting out of the car.

"You can pick me up anytime, stud."

Colin was in a great mood. In the last twenty-four hours, he had managed to have great sex with a young man, sex with his lover, and then spent the last few hours having his ego stroked by yet another very attractive man. Life didn't get much better than this. The best thing was yet to come, a whole day with his lover. That didn't happen too often. They needed to spend more time together. Strong as their relationship was, their busy schedules was placing an undue strain on it.

He stopped off at a local florist and picked out a great bunch of flowers to put in the bedroom. Then he went to the strip district and picked up an armful of Italian delicacies to cook on Saturday. If they were going to spend the day together, he was going to make it memorable. He might even take the phone off the hook so the hospital or the congregation didn't interfere.

When he got home, he found Millicent in Derek's office. Well, his exceptionally good luck had to end at some point. Millicent was about his age. She was short, petite, and very pretty with chestnut colored hair cascading around her face. "Hi Millicent, how are you doing?"

"Oh fine Colin, do you know where Derek is?"

"Yes," he deadpanned.

"Would you care to be a little more forthcoming with information?"

"He's at some dinner in town."

"Any clue what dinner and where?"

"Actually, I don't. Is there a problem?"

"I just needed to talk to someone," and with that, she almost seemed on the edge of tears.

Colin melted, "Is there anything that I can do for you?"

"Nothing that a divorce wouldn't cure. I'm at my wits end with him. He's cold and distant. He always yells at me for everything. I can't do anything right. I don't know what to do. I need to talk to Derek."

"You know, you should just make up your mind and divorce the guy. Get it over with and get on with your life," he said trying to be honestly sympathetic.

"It's a little easier for you guys, hopping from one relationship to another. . .

But before she could continue, Colin cut her off: "That's enough! I am so tired of you dismissing gay relationships as simply a walk in the park. They aren't. We do have feelings for each other, and we often get them hurt, and sometimes, there's a man that we just can't get over. How dare you be so blasé about the whole thing."

Millicent burst into tears and ran out of the room. Colin knew that he would pay for this one once she ratted on him to Derek. He would have to tell him, and probably the sooner the better. He would do it before they left for the bar. He knew that she was fragile, and he really shouldn't have challenged her, but, damn it! That didn't mean that she could walk all over him, or make his life seem less than authentic. He had spent too long working for gay rights to let someone dismiss his life and his right to form a loving and strong bond with another man.

Chapter 3

Derek arrived home in a great mood. Even the retelling of the Millicent incident didn't seem to phase him, although Colin merely alluded to it and didn't recount the entire argument, leaving some of the more damaging comments out. Colin was thanking his lucky stars for Derek's good mood and seemingly unconcerned attitude about his argument with Millicent. His lover was even excited about going out tonight. Derek was never excited about going out. This was due, at least in part, because they usually had to limit going to a bar to Friday nights because the good priest couldn't celebrate the liturgy with a hangover, at least not on a regular basis.

Colin was staring at his leather closet. He pulled out tonight's uniform: leather boots, chaps, and a vest. To this he would add black leather police gloves and a black leather biker cap. Each piece was put on carefully. It reminded him of the priest vesting for Mass. In a way, he was. Leather masters ruled the bar. Not only ruled, but presided over it, and the activities found there, often involving more ritual and protocol than any liturgy could possibly contain.

After his vesting was complete, he looked hot – in both senses of the word. Derek came over in boots, jeans, and a leather vest and knelt in front of him. Colin put the leather collar around his neck and locked it securely in place. It was this ritual that he liked the most in their relationship. It reaffirmed to him that whatever happened during the rest of the day or even week, this man would submit to him on some level.

When Derek got up, Colin tenderly kissed him on the mouth. That would be the last tender expression of love until they had completed sex the way that both of them liked it: rough. Colin had told Derek about Vlad a little earlier, and he seemed anxious to meet him. They swung by Vlad's house. He was already peering out the window, waiting for them. He came bounding down the sidewalk and all that

Derek could say was: "WOW!" It was true, as hot as Vlad looked that afternoon in the restaurant, he was amazing in leather.

"Hello, Sir, thank you for picking me up," he said as he entered the car. Then, following the strict leather protocol that all three men knew, he added, "May I speak to the boy?"

"Of course, let me introduce you. Vlad, this is my boy, Derek. Boy, this is Dr. Vlad Vostik."

"Hello, Sir," replied Derek.

"I'm no sir, I'm just as much of a boy as you are," Vlad said as he turned around and offered his hand to the man sitting quietly in the back seat.

The three men talked and laughed as Colin made his way through the city. The *Pirate's Nest* was located on top of a hill over-looking the downtown section of Pittsburgh. The area was called the Hill District and, while at one time it was a wealthy neighborhood, it was now a dangerous, run-down part of town. The bar itself managed to have a parking lot, which was surrounded by a large chain link fence. The owner, Brandon Mantune, called Brandy by everyone he knew, was often seen patrolling the perimeter. Legend had it that he always carried a gun with him. He was in the parking lot when the trio pulled in—smiling and waving as they got out of the car. Brandy could only be described as sleazy and washed out. Maybe, at one time, he had been attractive, but you certainly couldn't tell that now. These days he was just a pasty faced man with bad hair and the general appearance of being unkempt.

"My, it seems to be the three most handsome men in the city," he yelled with a smirk that came off more lecherous than flirtatious.

"Hello Brandy," was all that Colin responded.

"Don't tell me that you are going out tonight with two boys in tow, when the rest of us can't get any," Brandy said as he stopped between the guys and the door.

"Vlad isn't my boy," replied Colin.

"At least not yet," the doctor added.

Colin didn't see it, but when Vlad answered Brandy with that reply, Derek actually got a look of jealousy on his face, and consciously or unconsciously, stepped between Derek and Vlad. Had Colin seen it, he might not have believed it. Derek simply never showed any signs of jealousy.

They made their way into the darkened bar. The usual people

were sitting around because it was early. There was no sign of Dirk yet. He was always late for dates and appointments. Colin turned to Vlad and Derek and said, "I've been seeing the same people, wearing the same leather, sitting or standing in the same places for too many years now. We either need a new bar, or new blood in this bar."

Colin went to the bar and exchanged a few pleasantries with Brian, the bartender. They had the same routine each time that they met, a playful flirtation that never went anywhere. He ordered and got the drinks and gave Derek and Vlad theirs. It wasn't long before Dirk Szcemirski entered the bar. He was dressed in brand new leather literally from head to toe, and wore a large sash over his shoulder. On the sash, printed in rivets, was MR. STEEL CITY LEATHER, a title that he won at the local leather contest a couple of months before. Until that contest, he was a relatively normal kind of guy. After that, all he talked about was the leather contest circuit that he now found himself on, telling everyone that he hoped to become Mr. World Leather or whatever the current ultimate title was called. No one really knew the circuit, primarily because they didn't care, and whenever anyone (namely Dirk or Brandy) tried to tell them about it they just got a blank look on their face and zoned out for a while.

Colin, not approving of the attention that these contests got, greeted his old friend, "Well, if it isn't the newest sash queen in the leather world."

"You just wish that you had won a contest, don't you?" Replied Dirk.

"Actually no, I haven't even entered one. As a matter of fact, I never went to one until you were a contestant."

"You're just jealous," Dirk replied as he looked over at the corner where Derek and Vlad were having a conversation., "I see that you have met and conquered Vlad."

"He's not conquered, I just gave him a ride to the bar."

The rest of the evening at the bar involved Colin standing around Vlad and Derek, while the trio watched the various men make attempts at coupling. All the while, Dirk was greeting everyone who entered the bar, often acting up in such as way that Colin just looked on in disgust.

It was getting late and Colin was the first to suggest leaving, offering either to take Vlad back home or leave him to find a trick for himself. Surprisingly enough, it was Derek that suggested that Vlad might be interested in coming home with them and visiting that special place in the basement that the two lovers had set aside as a play area. Vlad was certainly agreeable to the idea, and while Colin wanted to spend a little time alone with Derek, he couldn't resist the Ukrainian's dark sensuous looks. In no time at all, they were back at the house.

Derek managed to prepare the dungeon area before the other two got downstairs. There were several candles lit around the periphery. On one wall was a St. Andrew's cross, not used for any religious ceremonies, but with restraints dangling from the top and at the bottom to bind the hands and feet of the person who was placed on the cross. There was a sling near the other wall. Most of the floor was covered with what looked to be a black wrestling mat.

Colin, still in full leather, found the two men, naked and kneeling on the floor when he entered. He stood between them and indicated that they should start licking his boots. Each man took a boot and bathed it with his tongue. Before long, Colin's erection could be seen through the jeans under his chaps. The erections of Derek and Vlad were readily noticeable the moment that Colin had entered the room.

Colin went over to the wall and took down a leather hood. He placed it gently on Derek's head and strapped the man to the cross. Then, as Vlad continued kneeling on the floor, Derek pulled down a flogger from the wall and begins whipping his lover. He started, gently at first, and then, after a while he was really hitting him hard and he could hear Derek's muffled cries from under the hood with its gag.

Colin then went over to Vlad and pulled out his dick telling the man to suck it. Vlad gladly took Colin's dick in his mouth and went to it. Colin stopped him after a while, not wanting to cum just yet. He went over, removed the hood from Derek, and untied him. His lover crumpled to the floor, as was so often the case when a man had really been flogged on the cross.

Colin then told Vlad to get into the sling. He tied his lover to the opposite wall and secured a gag around his mouth. As he prepared Vlad to be fisted he could see the absolute desolation in his lover's eyes. Colin had never fisted Derek, and he knew that he wanted it—but it simply wasn't time. As Colin worked his hand into the other man's ass, his lover pleaded with his eyes. This was total humiliation.

The truth was that Colin tired of fisting relatively easily. While the power trip was incredible, his focus was always on his own dick.

When he grew tired, he ordered Vlad to untie Derek and fuck him, which the man did readily. But Colin stopped them both before either of them reached climax, stepping in where Vlad just was, and finishing the job. He instructed Vlad to go around and feed Derek his cock while Colin continued to fuck him. In the end, all three men came at about the same time.

After they had all taken showers, Vlad offered to return to his home, but Colin insisted that they just go to sleep. The one thing that Colin brought from his condominium was his king-size Mission-style bed, and he loved it. They all climbed in together and before long, they were asleep.

The next morning, Colin woke up as Vlad was stroking Derek. Without the elaborate ritual of the night before, all three managed to get off once again. They then shared breakfast, and Vlad, knowing that Colin and Derek needed some time alone, begged off a sightseeing trip around the city and returned home.

As Colin was driving back with Derek, he restarted the telling of his confession of the argument with Millicent, hoping that an analysis of the scene would make it seem less important.

"I've already heard about it from her," Derek interrupted. "You should be a little more understanding. I know that she can be a little bitchy at times, but it's her husband, Michael, he's a real pain in the ass, and abuses her mentally most of the time."

"I don't understand why she doesn't just leave him."

"It might not be that easy for a priest, especially a woman priest. They haven't been around all that long, and parishioners tend to be a little more critical of them, at least, some parishioners. Give her a little leeway here. I suppose inviting her and Michael to dinner tonight is out of the question."

"Completely."

Derek knew not to pursue the issue any longer. He knew that special sound in Colin's voice that meant that the issue was dead, at least in Colin's mind. He also knew that they needed some time alone together. He would just have to console Millicent on Monday morning after Colin left for work. Perhaps a major breakfast somewhere followed by a Monday morning free from the parish office work.

The day went on wonderfully, with Colin preparing a great dinner that night. The meal was followed by watching a rented movie and then each man fell asleep while reading—Derek, a fantasy novel, and

Colin, yet another piece of trite gay fiction.

Since the weekend went so wonderfully, Derek decided that, as best as could be arranged, he and Colin would spend Saturdays together like this. And that's the way that it went for the next couple of months. Vlad was often a guest in their bed and in the downstairs 'room of special purpose', as Colin referred to the dungeon. Millicent continued to have problems with her husband, and Colin would, from time to time, visit Billy in his apartment.

Vlad, Derek, Colin and Billy managed to plan an out-of-town trip to Washington, DC together in January and were eagerly looking forward to it, even though Christmas was not yet near. They would go for Mid Atlantic Leather, a weekend dedicated to sensual delights, and a contest to pick the contestant who would represent the area at the next level of leather contests. None of them could wait to be in a hotel with a couple of thousand of other leather men. It was something for them to look forward to—even though it was still a ways off.

Chapter 4

As Christmas approached, Millicent became more morose, and more present in the Colin-Derek household. Well, after all, it was a rectory, and she was the curate. She had been married to Michael for about ten years. He was a brooding academic, with tenure at one of the local universities. He didn't like it that his wife was a priest. Colin thought that it was because it made her seem like more of a star in some domain, albeit, a domain that was only one day a week for most of the parish. Michael didn't like her bond with Derek either, but of course, Michael didn't like much. As Christmas approached, Michael's mood became darker, with Millicent subsequently becoming more needy. As Millicent became more needy, Michael got angrier, Colin became more frustrated, and Derek became more torn between these two important people in his life.

"My parents are coming for Christmas this year, is that all right?" Derek asked as Colin was getting ready for work.

"Of course, I always am happy to have them here for the holidays."

"I was thinking of asking Millicent and Michael over for dinner on Christmas day."

"That would probably be a good idea, I'm sure that Michael doesn't want to cook and you and Millicent are usually pretty busy from Advent on," Colin surprised himself at how understanding he was becoming. Part of that had to do with Derek devoting a day a week to him, part of it had to do with Vlad's continued attentions, and part had to do with Billy's periodic calls for company.

"I think that we should invite Vlad over as well, I doubt that he will be going to the Ukraine for the holidays," Colin added quickly.

"Don't you think that he is becoming too much a part of this relationship?" Derek asked, trying with all of his might not to sound bitchy, especially since Colin was being so understanding about Millicent.

"Actually I don't. We've had people in and out of this relationship before, and it didn't seem to exact any toll. Are you threatened by him?"

"Not really. Well, you go a lot further with him than you do with me, but even that's not it. I guess I was just being weird, it's only right to invite him over. Otherwise he'll be at Brandy's bar for the saddest Christmas dinner on record."

"Don't worry. No man is going to come between you and me. It's just not worth it."

"And, if Vlad were a top, and I liked him, and invited him over as much, would you be so understanding?" Derek added, making a mental note to kick himself because he really was becoming bitchy now.

"If I'm not mistaken, he's had that big Ukrainian dick up your ass quite a few times, and you seemed to like it. As a matter of fact, you liked it a lot."

"I know, let's just drop it."

Colin knew at that point that Vlad had indeed become too close to them in their relationship. It probably wasn't the sex so much as it was the intimacy that he and Colin shared after sex. Derek went to a different world after sex, a world with a high wall that no one could penetrate. Colin and Vlad, on the other hand, reveled in the afterglow of sexual fulfillment. Colin had long ago learned to deal with Derek's distance after sex. While it could be disconcerting at times, it didn't mean that the man was upset or angry with his lover. Derek, if asked, couldn't put into words what happened to him after sex. Usually sex with Colin was one of two kinds: intense and rough or tender and quick, the difference between a formal meal and a quick lunch. Being the bottom in a S/M scene could sometimes rob the person of his identity, at least for a little while. Derek just needed a little time to get it back. It wasn't that he resented Colin's attempted intimacy after sex, or even that he didn't want it. He simply couldn't respond. He would watch with envy as Vlad and Colin would kiss and cuddle when they all went to bed together.

The days leading up to Christmas passed quickly, with only a couple more days until the Wilsons arrived to celebrate Christmas with their son, the priest, and his lover. They were a fun couple with Mrs. Wilson, born and bred in England, the hardest to befriend. She was a true Brit, showing little emotion, and appearing at times, cold. But she loved her son, and seemed to like Colin. Mr. Wilson was a typical businessman, always making his trips an inspection of Colin and Derek's finances and retirement funds. They always stayed exactly eight days, from December 23 through December 30. It was as if they knew that Colin and Derek celebrated the Christmas holiday with the religious fervor that it should have and celebrated their sexuality at the year's end. Mrs. Wilson knew that Colin had, not only Welsh, but Scottish blood in him as well. Furthermore, she knew that a second-generation Scotch descendant still had the pagan year's end celebration as part of his identity. The Scotch always had been a little pagan about the end of December.

"Colin, have you seen Derek?" Millicent asked with a sense of urgency.

"No, I'm sorry, I haven't. Is there something I can do for you?"

"I don't think so. The choir director just called, he has the flu. Christmas is in two days, Michael is being totally awful, and I got my period."

"Well, a little more information than I needed. Look, you seem like you need a diversion. I'm on my way to pick up Derek's parents at the airport. Would you like to come along for the ride. We can watch the planes take off and land."

"Beware of Trojans bearing gifts," the priest added. "You probably want to throw me off the Fort Pitt bridge or something and tell the world that I was despondent and did it myself."

"I will grant you Millicent, that there are times when that would be at the top of my 'things to do' list, but I was just trying to be helpful."

"I know Colin, I'm just at my wits end."

"Well, does the choirmaster have a physician? If he doesn't I can get someone at the hospital to see him. And, if you would like, I could arrange for a counselor for you or Michael or both."

"That is sweet of you. Really, the Christmas season really does you good Colin. I'll call the choirmaster and see. Michael would never go to counseling, and I probably need a priest more than a counselor."

As Millicent went her way, Colin jumped into the Cherokee and headed for the airport. He managed to make it just as the Wilsons got out of the plane. They stopped off on the way home for a bite to eat, Colin not sure of Derek's schedule for the evening, and the Wilsons having spent all day long on a series of planes that only served them graham crackers all the way across the country.

Derek was home when they got there and Colin helped with the luggage and came down to make drinks for everyone. He stayed, talking to the family for about an hour, then begged off, saying that he had some work to do. Actually, he was trying to give Derek some time alone with his parents. They didn't see each other all that often, and, while they were accepting of their son's choice in a marriage partner, they didn't need to only see him when he was attached to that partner.

Colin and Mrs. Wilson spent Christmas Eve day preparing the evening meal and getting ready for Christmas dinner the next day. Mr. Wilson spent his time erecting the tree and going through Colin and Derek's finances. Derek, of course, was busy in the church, and with Millicent who had another personal crisis the evening of the Wilsons arrival.

The late service on Christmas Eve at St. Swithen's was beautiful. There was something about a small Episcopal church that made it seem just right for Christmas Eve. Colin was proud of Derek as he presided over his congregation which included Billy and Vlad. Tomorrow afternoon, he hoped that Derek would spend a quiet afternoon at home, and rest up a little. He and Mrs. Wilson had prepared a feast. He was a little nervous about Vlad coming. Not about how to introduce him, that was easy enough, a colleague at work, but about the intimacy that could betray the fact that they were more than just colleagues.

The morning service finished about noon and Derek was back at the rectory by one. Colin told Millicent, Michael and Vlad to show up at three. Dinner would be served at four. That gave a couple of hours for the exchange of presents before people arrived, and a little time for Christmas cheer before sitting down to dinner. Colin hoped that everything would be over by eight so Derek could get some well-deserved rest.

Millicent arrived first, without Michael, who Millicent informed them would be coming along shortly. He managed to arrive at the door the same time as Vlad did, eyeing him critically.

"Merry Christmas, damnable weather we're having," Michael grumbled as he entered the room.

"Merry Christmas everybody!" Vlad countered with all of the joy that Christmas should evoke. Sometimes he shocked everyone with his wide-eyed wonder, much like that of a small child.

"Millicent made a mess of breakfast this morning, and I can tell by the smell of things that we're in for a good meal. Of course, with two homosexuals in the house, the meal should be good," Michael continued while making himself a drink.

Millicent turned away and walked into the kitchen, making some excuse about helping Mrs. Wilson. The rest of the party stood still, with Michael's words lying before them like the excrement of a bad dog. Colin took the lead, and changed the subject.

"How are things at the university, Michael?"

"It gets harder every year. I tell you, if I would have known what was in store for me when I started out, I wouldn't be there. I would be where the money is, industry, or, like you, health care."

"Well, health care has it's own problems. I think that you know everyone except Vlad. Dr. Michael Barclay meet Dr. Vlad Vostik."

The two men shook hands and began a conversation about where Vlad was from and what he did. The rest of the party breathed a sigh of relieve. Derek went into the kitchen and found his mother consoling Millicent. Asking if he could be of assistance, his mother answered only, "Serve wine Derek, and lot's of it. We'll get some Christmas cheer into this day yet."

All in all, the dinner went well. Michael eventually calmed down, and was even a little nice to Millicent. Vlad was the life of the party and everyone seemed to like him. By eight o'clock Derek looked as if he could drop. Colin gave Vlad the high sign and he politely said his good-byes. Millicent and Michael took their cue as well and left. As Colin and Mrs. Wilson continued to clean up a little, Derek had some time alone with his father, which didn't happen all that often.

"Are you happy, son?" The elder Wilson asked.

"Of course, I'm happy. It's Christmas."

"I mean, in general, are you happy? That's what a parent wants most for their child."

"Well, Pittsburgh isn't the greatest place to be when you are like me. I mean, it's not bad, but there are better places to live."

"Any chance of you moving?" His father asked.

"I assume that we will soon. I've only been at the parish for a little over four years. I should stay a couple more. I know that Colin is looking. We'll just have to see how it will play out."

"And if one or the other can't find a job?"

"I hope that doesn't happen, but we would have to decide on which way to go. Colin is open to taking a lower position, but he makes a lot more money that I ever will."

"Well, I hope that it works out for you two."

Just then, Mrs. Wilson and Colin brought in some more deserts and coffee. "Just thought we could unwind a little after the company left," she said in her best English accent.

"I sure hope that the coffee is decaffeinated," was Mr. Wilson's reply.

"Of course, we're all tired," she answered her husband.

After the final desert, everyone agreed that it was time to call it a day. As Colin slipped into the sheets with his lover, he leaned over and kissed him on the mouth.

"Well, we've managed another year together."

"Were you of the understanding that we wouldn't make it?" Derek replied with a smile.

"No, but sometimes a boy just needs a little reinforcement."

Before either one could continue the conversation, they both drifted off to sleep. The next few days went by quickly, Derek's time taken up with his family. Colin cut back his schedule at work to be with them as much as possible. Finally, the day for their departure arrived and, as quickly as they entered into their lives, they were gone. Derek always was a little down after his parents left, even though a week with them was enough. He liked having people in the house, but he liked his privacy as well. He also liked the routine that he and Colin had, although he wouldn't admit to it. Colin wasn't always that easy to live with. When a man has great passion, he has good deal of emotion to go with it. Sometimes it was hard to deal with all of that emotion. However, in the end, life with Colin was more fun than without him. Derek knew that Colin was very understanding in some areas, and a little volatile in others. He had known his lover long enough to know what pressed his buttons—both his on and his off buttons.

The New Year Eve celebration found Colin, Derek, Vlad, and Billy all at the *Pirate's Nest*. Granted it wasn't a gala event. Brandy was his usual sleazy self, and Dirk seemed to be the resident person in charge since he won that contest. But, the four of them were looking forward to the big MAL party in DC in a couple of weeks. They were reconciled to celebrating the New Year in a tacky bar on top of a hill in Pittsburgh in a very bad section of town with a bunch of losers didn't seem like the end of the world. Dirk did his usual attempt at getting either Vlad or Billy into bed with him. Neither were inclined to accept his offers, knowing full well, that all four of them would be playing in Colin and Derek's basement before the New Year had seen the first light of day.

Chapter 5

When he had arrived early at the hospital that January Thursday morning, it had not yet begun to snow, although you could tell that it was about to begin. The sky in Pittsburgh that morning was a slate gray blue that cast an eerie glow on everything. Since it was winter, there were no leaves on the trees. From the hill top vantage point of the hospital parking lot, you could see over many neighborhoods, from the Oakland section all the way into the tall buildings of the center of the city. It was easy to forget how green Pittsburgh really was, until the dead of winter, when it was all gone, and neighborhoods were no longer hidden from each other.

It began to snow shortly after that, and continued snowing heavily all morning long. Colin was a little distressed. He and Derek were supposed to pick up Billy and leave that night after work for DC. They were driving, meeting Vlad, who was flying there and then onto a conference after the big leather weekend. It wasn't that Colin was afraid to drive in the snow, but the mountains between Pittsburgh and DC could get a little difficult in bad weather. They had all been looking forward to this weekend for a long time. Derek needed a weekend away from St. Swithen's. Colin also needed the weekend away, but wished that he was going alone with Derek. That was OK, he had already checked with Millicent, and he and Derek were going to spend a weekend in a cabin alone in about a month, the middle of February. It would be a surprise for his lover. However, today he would call Derek and see if they could leave a little earlier in the day from their planned departure time.

"Derek, do you think we could leave a little bit early, if I can get out of here?" Colin sounded more flustered than usual.

"Of course, but what about Billy?"

"I'll give him a call. If he can make it, I'll swing by and maybe we will be able to leave about two."

"OK, I'll wait for you."

As it turned out, Billy was just sitting by the phone waiting for the day to end and the trip to begin. He jumped at the chance when Colin said that they could leave early. By two o'clock that afternoon they were inching their way to Washington—inching because the roads were almost impassable. It took them almost seven hours to make a four-hour trip, but they arrived at their hotel at nine o'clock that night. Nothing was happening on Thursday night, so they would have the ability to rest up, go to the airport and meet Vlad the next day and be ready for the weekend festivities.

The suite was wonderful. They weren't staying at the host hotel, it was just too crowded and noisy. They were right down the street, and the accommodations were great. After a quick late night dinner, they were back in the room, sprawled out on the big bed. Derek and Billy were being unusually affectionate with one another. Colin felt a little pang of jealousy, wondering why his lover was not as demonstrative with him. They all three played around a little and fell asleep long before one in the morning.

The next day, Billy volunteered to take the car to the airport to pick up Vlad. That gave Colin and Derek the morning to stroll around Dupont Circle. They both loved it here, and, given half the chance, would probably be willing to relocate.

"I'm shocked that you trusted Billy with the car," Derek marveled over a muffin in one of the coffee shops.

"Why? He's really a responsible boy. He just doesn't seem to have any direction in his life," Colin responded, adding, "By the way, you two were really chummy last night."

"Are you jealous? As many times as you've had your dick up his ass?"

"Not really jealous. Let's just say envious."

With that, Derek reached across the table and kissed his lover on the mouth. Then he held on to his hand while they were talking. Colin was amazed.

"What's gotten in to you?' He asked.

"Sometimes I just need to get out of Pittsburgh to be open and free again. Pittsburgh represents tension to me. I mean, there's the crazy bishop on my case most of the time, then the little fights that you and Millicent are having, and on every corner there's a guy that you have slept with at one time or another. It's just a little oppressive at times. Not to mention that there is absolutely no visible gay community there."

Once Derek had said the words he regretted it, fearing that Colin would take it as the opening salvo of another battle. He didn't. He simply looked at his lover, lowered his head and replied, "I know. Sometimes I forget how hard it is for you there, and I'm not exactly patient with Millicent. Trust me, say the word, and when you're ready to leave, we can do it."

The rest of the morning was spent visiting shops. Of course, Lambda Rising was on the agenda, not that they could put one more book anywhere in their house. Then, it was on to the leather shop to see what they could use before they visited the leather emporium that would be around the contest site. After a leisurely lunch they returned to the hotel, expecting to find Billy and Vlad.

Billy greeted them with the news that Vlad was not on the plane. Colin thought that it was unusual. Even more unusual that Vlad didn't call. If there was an emergency, that was understandable, but he was sure that Vlad would have called if he couldn't make it. He picked up his cell phone and called Vlad's cell phone, leaving a message to please call when he was able. Derek saw the look of concern on Colin's face, but reassured him that Vlad was either operating on someone, or had managed to find the trick of his life and was 'tied up' for a while, making reference to Vlad's fondness for elaborate bondage scenes.

Not dwelling on the issue, the three showered, shaved, and began the vesting ritual that leather men all over the world do in one form or another. When they were ready it looked as if a motorcycle club had hit the room. Colin was in leather jeans and boots with a motorcycle jacket and cap with black police gloves. Derek wore his jacket with a locked collar and boots with jeans, while Billy was a mirror image, only without the lock. The collar on both boys signified that they 'belonged' to Colin. The lock on Derek's collar told the rest of the leather men that he was not free to play without his master. Billy's unlocked collar represented the fact that he could play with his master's permission. These were all old guard leather rules that Colin knew like the back of his hand. Both Billy and Derek were fond of the old guard ritual, up to a point, even though they were both too young to have experienced it first hand.

They went over to the hotel and entered a lobby with about two thousand men, clad in much the same way as they were. Of course, there was the usual smattering of military uniforms, and police uniforms, and an occasional hot stud in a leather kilt, but black leather was definitely the theme. Colin was a little distressed that there were so many women here this year. Not that he minded women, but he didn't want them in his play space.

After paying fifteen dollars for three drinks, the trio went into the arcade where any sort of leather equipment could be found, for a price. They had a great time, seeing old friends from past years, looking at the leather goods, and marveling at what was offered for their amusement.

It wasn't long before they saw Dirk standing with Brandy, talking about something in hushed tones. When Colin walked up to them, they looked a little tense.

"Hey guys, what's up? Have you seen Vlad, by any chance?" Colin asked as he approached them.

"You don't know?" Dirk asked.

"Know what?" Colin responded.

"Vlad is dead. The police found him in his room. They said that it was suicide, that he asphyxiated while masturbating," Brandy interjected.

Colin was dumbfounded. He wished that Derek was at his side, but he and Billy were nowhere to be found. He couldn't believe that Vlad was dead. It wasn't that he thought that his friends and sexual partners couldn't be dead, he had come of age during the AIDS epidemic. It was just that he couldn't believe someone would die so suddenly, and somewhat cruelly. The bottom line was that Colin couldn't believe that Vlad could kill himself, either intentionally or by accident.

"How was he found?" Colin managed to blurt out.

"One of his colleagues went to meet him this morning to go to the airport. When they didn't get an answer, they tried the door and found him upstairs, dead, with a rope around his neck," Dirk answered while putting his arm around a visibly shaken Colin. Brandy didn't have anything else to add.

Colin had more questions to ask, but just couldn't manage to form them. He excused himself from Dirk and Brandy and went to look for Billy and Derek. It didn't take long, he found them admiring a display of various sizes of dildos in various colors, made of various materials, including a large chrome one that Billy seemed particularly fond of.

Derek could see that something was troubling Colin right away.

"What's wrong?" He asked.

"Could you and Billy come outside with me for a minute?"

The three men made there way through the throng of leather-clad men. When they reached the door, Colin led them toward their hotel.

"Vlad's dead. They think that it was either suicide or a masturbation scene gone bad."

Derek and Billy just looked stunned. It was as if the words didn't sink in, and they were not comprehending what Colin just told them. Derek was the first to comment, "How did they find him and what made them come to that conclusion?"

Colin answered, "One of his co-workers found him. They were supposed to be picking him up to go to the airport. The door was unlocked. When they didn't get an answer, they walked in. He was apparently upstairs, dead, with a rope around his nick."

"But he's a doctor, he wouldn't do that to himself, and he was so happy," Billy added, seeming to use logic to prove the information that he just received was false.

"I'm not sure Billy, but, unless Dirk and Brandy are playing a really sick joke, Vlad is dead. I'm sure that they are not joking, you know how they love to gossip."

Derek finally took control, "Look guys, I don't feel much like partying. There's not a lot that we can do, let's go get out of this leather and take a quiet walk."

The three men made their way back to the hotel room, changed into the usual gay man drag: jeans, T-shirts, and black leather jackets with black boots. They started walking toward Dupont Circle. They walked for what seemed like hours, finally making their way to Annie's Paramount Steak House. There they drank a little too much, and then ate a little too much. By the end of the dinner they weren't in shock any more. Granted, they didn't feel like partying that night, but they weren't about to rush home to Pittsburgh either. After all, not one of them was family, in the strict interpretation of the word. There wasn't too much that any of them could do. Colin knew that there would be a coroner's inquiry into the cause of death, and bodies weren't shipped out of the country over night.

By the time that they got back to the hotel, they changed into their leathers again and joined the festivities at the local leather bar. It was so crowded that it was almost comic. They couldn't get a drink, and couldn't move around, so basically, they couldn't do much. For some reason, the three of them found it extremely funny and started laughing at everything. For once, Colin broke his stern leather Master-routine in a leather bar.

After having too much to drink and staying out way too late in the night, they found themselves all in bed playing around, but not really into a major leather scene. It's amazing how death seems to make everyone horny. The sex was good, they all came about the same time and then fell asleep.

The next day they decided that they *would* participate in the whole leather weekend in Vlad's memory. Since they hadn't participated in the revelries which lasted until dawn, they were surprisingly fresh, and not quite as jaded as their comrades on the weekend. While Colin loved the energy of leather weekends, he often found them just a little boring. How much shopping can you do? How many leather floggers does a person need? Standing around and drinking very expensive drinks got old as well. Perhaps it was just because of Vlad's death, but he didn't really seem into the whole thing. He and Derek found some time to sneak off and be by themselves again. Funny, when a crowd surrounded them, they sought to be alone to find solace in one another. When they were alone at home, they looked for ways to invite others into their shared solitary life. Such was human nature. Relationships had been destroyed over two people refusing to acknowledge human nature, but Colin and Derek seem to celebrate it.

As they were getting comfortable in a coffee shop on Connecticut Avenue, Dave, a friend from Pittsburgh, greeted and then joined them.

"How are you guys doing this weekend?" He began.

"We're having a good time. Basically because we've managed to get out of town," Derek replied, rising to embrace their friend.

"And you, how is your weekend going?" Colin inquired.

"Oh, I don't know. Sometimes it's just a little too much. I come to these things expecting so much, like I will find Mr. Right and settle down. Then I decide that it's all about sex and I assume that I am going to have the best sexual experience of my life. In the end, it turns out to be a hangover and a miserable trip back to the burgh," Dave answered, and quickly added, "I guess that you got more than you bargained for when you asked. Sometimes I give the long philosophical commentary to a question."

"No, not at all, Derek and I were discussing the same thing when you found us."

"Where's the boy toy?" Dave asked, referring to Billy.

"He found a body builder, and I'm sure that they are exploring each other's musculature right now," Derek responded.

"Did you guys hear about Vlad?" Dave asked.

"Yes, we did. Amazing. I can't believe it. I just saw him a few days ago." Colin answered.

"I just saw him Thursday night." Dave continued.

"You're kidding! He died either late Thursday or early Friday morning, where did you see him?" Derek asked.

"At the bar. He was there having a great time, drinking. He left with Dirk. Dirk must have been the last person to have sex with him."

"You mean that Dirk went home with Vlad?" Colin asked, incredulous that Dirk neglected to mention that fact when he told him about Vlad's death. After all, Dirk had been trying to get Vlad to have sex with him since Vlad first walked into that bar. "Funny, I just saw Dirk yesterday, and he didn't mention having sex with Vlad, only that he was dead."

"Maybe he didn't want you to accuse him of doing anything. Really Colin, Dirk is a moron, but he's a nice moron, there's not a vicious bone in his body. He wouldn't harm a flea," Dave said, although he was also confused that Dirk wouldn't have mentioned his encounter with Colin, they were friends. He knew that they had just seen each other at the hotel.

"Wouldn't harm a flea intentionally, but he's not very proficient. Nice and all, dumb as a stone, but totally inept when it comes to leather sex, and he thinks that he's a top," Colin was quick to add.

"With friends like you Colin, who needs enemies," his lover chided.

After a while, the three men got up to leave, Colin and Derek returning to their hotel while Dave went off to find the perfect man. Alone, on the street, Colin confided to Derek that he thought that Dirk might have started a scene that he didn't know how to handle, and that Vlad had died because of it. He felt that he had to confront Dirk.

"Colin, maybe you should wait, at least until we get home, to question Dirk."

"Why?"

"You don't want a public scene here. Besides, if it was an accident, what should happen to Dirk? It's not like these sorts of activities are licensed or anything, there isn't any legal standard of negligence for this. And remember, once you get information, you have to do something about it."

"I know, maybe I should just let it drop. The police are not exactly understanding about these things."

"Right and think how it would look. An auto mechanic who happens to be a friend of the local hospital administrator and his Episcopal priest lover, has inadvertently killed a world renown surgeon during an S/M sexual scene."

"Well, the Christian right would certainly love that. It would give them yet some more ammunition."

"Not to mention your enemies at the hospital and, lest we forget, the good Right Reverend Bishop of Pittsburgh."

"OK, point well taken. I'll just assume that it was a screw-up and that he's learned his lesson, besides, if I make myself present, he'll eventually spill the beans."

As Colin and Derek entered the lobby of their hotel, Dirk was pacing back and forth, looking very nervous, and very eager to talk to the two men.

"Will you guys take a walk with me?"

"Of course we will Dirk," Derek answered, knowing full well that he and Colin had been walking around Washington with heavy boots on most of the day. He would have to deal with his lover's complaints a little later. Everybody knows that there's nothing like sore feet to put someone in a grouchy mood.

"I want you guys to know something," Dirk began, "I kind of tricked with Vlad the night that he died, but he was very much alive when I left. Or, when I was asked to leave."

"What do you mean, you kind of tricked?" Colin asked.

"Well, we left the bar together, and we started once we got home, but, at one point, he told me that I was inept and said that we should stop."

"Have you told anyone else about this? And I should tell you, people saw you leaving with Vlad, and people will talk. If there is an investigation, it's only a matter of time before the police will know," Colin replied sternly.

"I know, I will definitely tell them when I get back to

Pittsburgh."

Derek couldn't stand it anymore. He looked squarely at Dirk and said, "Don't you think that they might be a little suspicious of a man who goes home with another guy who just happens to end up dead, and then the other man goes away for a four day orgy in the nation's capital?"

"I don't know what to do."

"Well, you said that it was initially ruled as a suicide, or something along those lines." Colin stated.

"That's what the rumor is."

"When we get back to the city, I'll make some inquiries. If there is any suspicion, you should go to the police and tell them. You're sure that you're telling me the truth."

"Yes Colin, it's the truth."

"One question Dirk, did you leave the door unlocked when you left?"

"I was taken to the door by Vlad, he wasn't too happy, telling me that I was totally useless to him sexually. He closed it, and I assumed that it was locked."

As the three men rounded the corner, the door to Derek and Colin's hotel was in front of them.

"Dirk, Colin and I need a little rest before the night, we're going to leave you now," Derek said.

"OK Derek, thanks for talking to me guys."

"No problem, but I've had Colin walking around in boots, and, if I don't get him off his feet for at least a couple of hours, I'll pay for it later."

"But I thought that you liked that," Dirk said returning to his old persona, then left the two lovers.

When they got upstairs, Derek removed Colin's boots and they both laid the across the bed. They were glad that Billy was still occupied. As tense as times could be in a gay relationship, there were those times when life was simply good. This was one of those times, not because anything major was happening, other than the death of a friend, but because they were so comfortable together. And now especially, since they were taking comfort from each other because of the news of Vlad's death. They often forgot that comfort when they were disagreeing about something. In many ways, their personalities matched those of the ill-fated royal lovers, Nicholas II of Russia and his wife Alexandra. Colin was definitely Nicholas, a strong willed man, filled with power, both sexually and in his employment. Nevertheless, the true strength came from Derek, who resembled Alexandra in the hold that he maintained over his lover's thoughts. They brought this same passion to their relationship, and while Colin held the visible reigns of power, it was Derek who often managed to make changes through his quiet, and sometimes, not so quiet influence. They played the usual games that all gay men played with their lovers, those psychological terrors that caused more harm than good, but, in the end, they always came back to the comfort of their relationship, and the love whose intensity maintained it.

The rest of the weekend was spent in subdued sexual abandon. They went to the parties, and even played around a little. Their true joy came from being out of Pittsburgh, and Colin realized that they really had to make some decisions about their place of living. Monday morning came and they packed up their leathers and Billy, and then began the drive back. A quick stop at the National Cathedral for Derek to regain some of his religious serenity was the first order of the day. Colin let Derek go off by himself for a couple of hours while he and Billy explored the various stairs and corners of the cathedral. Colin was amazed that he often forgot that his lover was a priest. Billy, for his part, could never comprehend it, and seemed to think that Derek was just pretending when he lead the liturgy or was present with a starched linen collar around his neck.

Chapter 6

In the weeks that passed, Colin and Derek fell back into their regular routine. Colin made some inquiries about Vlad's death after they had returned to Pittsburgh. Apparently, it was more of an embarrassment for local authorities than a crime to be investigated. The hospital asked that whatever investigation was started would be completed quickly, and quietly as possible. The coroner, a bumbling fool, but an acquaintance of Colin's told him the facts: Vlad was found upstairs in the bedroom, hands handcuffed behind his back, and a rope around his neck. He was naked. While the handcuffs caused a little concern, Colin knew plenty of bottoms that were very good at putting their hands in cuffs behind their backs and managing to get them off. Since the authorities had closed the case, and there wasn't any information to be had, he decided to drop it and get on with life. The only thing that really bothered him was the unlocked door. He had managed to convince Vlad to always check the door, because, while Shadyside was a good neighborhood, it was subject to random robberies. Primarily, because Pittsburgh was so old and so compact, good neighborhoods were often located right next door to bad neighborhoods.

It was only three weeks until the date of his and Derek's getaway when Colin discovered that he had to go to Columbus, Ohio for a meeting. Derek hated it when Colin had to go to Columbus, primarily because Colin's ex-lover, Tony, lived there. When Derek met Colin, it was right after their break-up and he felt that Colin never fully ended the thing. He hated it when Colin went to Columbus for anything, and Colin, for his part, tried to always arrange it so Derek could go along with him.

That night at home, Colin greeted his lover with a kiss and a proposition, "Hi, want to go to Columbus for a few days? We could leave on Thursday and come back Saturday night?"

"When?"

"This weekend."

"Colin, come on. You know that I can't leave on that short of notice. Why do you have to go?"

"Meeting at a hospital. I can't manage to get out of it."

"Don't they believe in a little notice?"

"Sorry Derek. I just found out. If you can't go, I could take Billy as a chaperone."

"Ummmm, a twenty-something little whore as a chaperone for my lover while he goes to the city where his ex-lover is languishing, unable to form another relationship since the love of his life left him......that's comforting."

"Well, with Billy you wouldn't have to worry about Tony. Actually, maybe they could get together."

"Colin, come on, if you want a big fuck-fest in Columbus just say it, don't make me feel that it's for my own good."

This was uncommon for Derek. He never seemed to have any sense of jealousy concerning his lover. Granted, Tony had been a problem early in their relationship. He always seemed to be calling and talking about subjects that were definitely pre-Derek. Then there was his insistence that he didn't want to meet Derek. Of course, there were the little ties that kept them together, a book left that had to be retrieved, a photo found, a friend's inquiry, and so on. Then finally there was the fact that Tony wouldn't or couldn't involve himself in another relationship. He and Colin had a long standing long distance relationship which had soured Colin on the whole idea of that sort of arrangement. Tony spent his days and nights in Columbus, working and picking up ever-younger boys who managed to last only a couple of weeks. He sat in bars or coffee shops on the Short North, looking dour until something under thirty came along and then he turned into an eighteenth century French courtesan. Derek could never figure out what Colin saw in him. After a few minutes of reflection, Derek decided that it just wasn't worth a fight, he could drop it, and spend a little quality time with Millicent during the absence.

"OK, I'm sorry. I'm just a little on edge. Millicent has been having a lot of problems with Michael. Go, have a great time. Taking Billy might be good. Maybe he can find a lover there, and get on with his life."

"I know that he has been a little intrusive lately. I hope that he finds someone. Maybe I can use this time to talk to him."

"You're a little in love with him, aren't you?"

"Derek, come on! I'm in love with you. Period. Billy's nice, but that's it, he's a nice kid. I don't want a relationship with him."

"But you don't mind fucking him, do you?"

"You've been there when I've fucked him. Come on Derek. Let's drop this. I'll either take him or leave him here, depending on what you say you want. I haven't even checked to see if he can go."

"Sorry Colin, it's just been a bad day. I'm a little on edge. Maybe we've added too many distractions in our relationship. And the Bishop is on my case again. I just wish we lived somewhere a little more gay friendly. And I'm finally upset about Vlad."

"Me too—maybe we could arrange a memorial for him. By the way, you certainly didn't mind Vlad fucking you, did you?"

Both men dissolved into laughter as they prepared dinner together. Colin always knew how to disarm a situation, although he sometimes didn't use his secret weapon. He loved the nights when they prepared dinner together and wasted a night without doing anything other than being an old married couple. It didn't happen all that often. Later that night Colin called Billy and invited him on the trip to Columbus. Billy accepted gladly. Derek got on the phone and gave Billy his orders: he was absolutely forbidden from taking Colin away from him. By the end of the evening, they had forgotten the previous tense moments.

"By the way, I had lunch today with the cute Roman priest from down the street," Derek started as they were about to go to bed. "You will never guess what is about to happen. Brandon Mantune is being awarded Papal Knighthood. It seems that he has given a lot of money to the church, and some good Roman Catholic Bishop of somewhere or the other is making him a knight of something or the other."

"You're kidding. I didn't even know that the man went to church. Doesn't anyone know that he owns a crappy gay bar in the middle of a black ghetto and that he waters down his liquor and charges too much, simply because it's the only leather bar in Pittsburgh?"

"And I doubt that the fact that he maintained a bar in a bad neighborhood would even figure in—the hierarchy haven't exactly been known for their concern over our safety and well-being. Apparently, when money is involved, none of that is important. You know that, you studied to be a Roman priest once. You know that the church will often overlook something in a person that can give them something else, namely money."

"Unfortunately I do. I don't condemn the church for that, after all, the church lives in the world and must function in the world. It's just that the man is to tacky."

"Well the good Father knows all about Brandy."

"Is he gay?"

"Yes, and cute as well. I know how you love Italian men. I've asked him to come to dinner when we come back from our weekend."

"So, I get to be the Rector's wife? How interesting."

By the time that they started discussing the menu for the good priest's dinner, Colin started getting playful, and before long, the two of them had made love and drifted off to sleep.

A couple of days later, Colin drove by Billy's apartment, picking him up and driving out to Columbus. Billy was excited. As worldly as he seemed, he had not really traveled far from Pittsburgh except for some rural college in the middle of the state. He was excited and started smoking a joint shortly after they got on Route 70 heading west.

"If we get stopped by the police, you're on your own dude," Colin said, always critical of Billy's recreational drug use.

"Come on dad, don't be such a weirdo," Billy replied, knowing that the dad comment always got Colin's goat.

"OK, I give up. And don't ever call me dad again."

In a few hours, the two men were already in Columbus. Colin was staying at a friend's condominium right on the Short North, the gay section of town. The Short North was a collection of galleries, shops, bars, restaurants, and coffee shops. Some of the business were gay owned and most of them were gay friendly. It was quite a cosmopolitan neighborhood for a city that was once known as cow town, and not too long ago. His friend, a psychiatrist, was out of town, and had mailed the key to Colin, telling him to keep it and always feel like he had a home in Columbus.

Within a few minutes of arriving, Billy dragged Colin down to the coffee shop owned by some lesbians to read the local gay papers and decide what was going on. Colin and Billy then spent the rest of the evening dropping by the local gay bookstore, visiting the various shops, and finally stopping by a gay video bar. It had quite a few televisions and a pool table in the back. The men there were all young, and hot. This was, in part due to the Ohio State influence, with so many undergraduates concentrated in a relatively small area.

"I want to go to the leather bars while I'm here," Billy stated.

"Of course, but can we wait until tomorrow night. Wednesday has never been particularly fun in a leather bar."

"Should I get a map, so we can find them?"

"No, I think that I can find them all on my own."

"Man Colin, you know your way around DC and Columbus?"

"And a few other cities as well. Billy, I've got an early meeting tomorrow. Do you mind if I call it a night? You can stay here, there are two keys, just don't get into any trouble."

"How about if I go home and you just fuck me senseless?"

"Well," Colin said with a sly smile on his face, "I thought that you would never ask."

The two men walked the short distance back to the condominium, and before long, Billy had his request fulfilled. Colin knew that Derek was right. He did have feelings for this kid. They weren't strong enough to pose any danger to his and Derek's relationship, but they did interfere. He would have to cut the boy loose soon. Colin secretly hoped that Billy would find someone on this trip and fall in love. Besides, there was fifteen years difference between the two of them. The ten years difference between him and Derek were enough of a generation gap to keep him on his toes. Of course, Colin had a feeling that Derek had been born a fully mature gay man, none of that foolish homosexual adolescence for him.

The next morning, Colin kissed Billy on the forehead, telling him that he would be home around five o'clock and that they could get dinner after that. Billy told him that he was planning on finding as much sex today as he could, and asked if the baths were within walking distance. As Colin left him, he told him to be careful. Boys in the leather world were often at the mercy of tops—some were proficient, and, some were not. Then there was that small segment of truly sadistic people out there who were ready, not only to hurt, but harm people as well, the psychos.

The day for Colin was filled with meetings, boring meetings. Colin wondered if Derek would like it in Columbus, better than Pittsburgh. He didn't know what the Episcopal church was like here, but he was sure that the vitality of the gay community would be a bonus. It was just that the medical community here was presiding over a system that was about to collapse in on itself. Pittsburgh had gone through a restructuring of its medical institutions a few years ago. Columbus still was maintaining an older system that no longer worked in the current environment of cost-containment and managed care. If Derek could get a job, maybe he could just hang out and look for another career. He would bring it up to Derek when he got back.

That evening, Billy and Colin had dinner in a place that presented itself as a Scottish bar/restaurant and was decorated accordingly. Colin, familiar with things Scottish, was skeptical about the Scottish connection. But it did have good bar food, and that was the cuisine that Billy liked most. It was interesting, sitting here with an attractive blond haired, blue-eyed man. Colin could see that he was the envy of many of the customers. They were a mixed bag. Some were tables of overly developed OSU jocks, while there were a couple of tables of men that were obviously drag queens, out of drag. Then there were several tables with two people seated at each, one a gay man and the other, a woman of a certain age, and often of a certain girth, enjoying a meal together. The men were always stylish, while the women were often not. The gay men at these tables spoke softly while the women's voices carried, and their laughter resonated throughout the bar. Colin could never understand the need that some gay men had to include women in their lives, especially women who were usually rejected by straight men for one reason or another. Maybe it was because they shared in the experience of the exclusion of straight men.

"Come on Billy, I'll buy you desert at the coffee shop."

When they walked into the coffee shop, there was Tony, sitting dour and sullen, looking very much like the world had been cruel to him and that he aware of every injury that had been heaped upon him.

"Tony, nice to see you," Colin said as he stood by the man's table.

"Oh, it's Mr. Wonderful. Should I stand up? What's the matter, the priest boy get a little too old for you, who is the new Mrs. Morgan here?"

"Oh sorry. Tony, this is Billy; Billy, this is Tony. We were once lovers. Billy is a friend. Derek is still my spouse, he just couldn't make the trip."

"And he let you come here, to the lion's den? Amazing! Doesn't he think that you and I are going to go at it again? As if I would ever let that happen."

"Derek's busy this weekend. Have a nice evening Tony, we have to get some coffee."

"Billy," Tony continued, "Be careful of this man—he breaks people's hearts then he just walks on by."

Billy didn't know what to say or do. He stood there and smiled benignly. Colin got coffee and cookies and took him to a far corner of the coffee shop.

"Boy, he's a mess," was all that the young man could say.

"Yes, he is. Actually he always was."

"I can't believe that you two were together. You're so not alike."

"Sometimes opposites attract and it works, sometimes it turns into a disaster."

"How long were you two together?"

"For ten years."

"Man, that's a long time to be with a disaster."

"Billy, I have a fear that I have never let anyone in on. I'm afraid of being alone. When you're a gay man, that's a pretty realistic fear. If we don't have someone by the time that we're forty, we often don't get anyone. When I turned thirty I thought that I was old. And now, forty for me is right around the corner."

"I know. I can't believe that I'm a almost quarter of a century old already."

Colin knew that he shouldn't laugh, but he did. He was amazed when someone in their twenties thought that they were getting so old. He wondered what he would be like when he turned forty, or, even more scary, when he turned fifty. He hoped that he would still be with Derek. He hoped that they would be somewhere else. Hopefully, they would be happy.

The next night, Colin took Billy to a tacky looking leather bar. It wasn't like the bar in Pittsburgh, there were more people here. But it wasn't unlike the bar in Pittsburgh, it was just a tiny space decorated in the same style as all leather bars, with the same type of people milling around the cruise areas. Colin adopted his stern quiet leather top look, standing in the shadows and staring down cute boys. He could always amaze Derek with his ability to stare at someone and draw them to himself, much like the vampires in old horror films. Billy looked like he was having fun, and it was with a man that Colin had seen on many of his trips to Columbus. He thought that Billy would be safe with this man. Colin surprised himself by not participating extensively in the courting ritual of the bar. When Billy came over and told him that he was going home with his new found conquest, Colin smiled, watched them leave, and then left himself, going back to the condominium and curled up with a book. Maybe he really was an old married man. And it didn't feel all that bad to him.

Saturday's meetings were mercifully short and he and Billy went shopping, buying small gifts for Derek. Kind of like a Christmas in February thing. Billy was going to go out to dinner with his trick from last night so Colin was on his own. He went to a movie alone at the Lennox Center, or what he always called, 'the pleasure dome'. It was one of those mega-movie houses with tons of movies showing in many smaller theatres contained under one roof.

Sunday morning he left a note for Billy and thought that he would check out the church situation in Columbus. He found a small Episcopal church on the East side of town, St. Peter's. The East side of Columbus must have been quite a neighborhood at one time. It was filled with rambling, big, old Victorian houses, many now having fallen into disrepair. However, there was a spark of life—many were being restored, and the number of gay flags were an indication to Coin that it would probably become one of those wonderful gay owned, restored neighborhoods that all large cities had.

He went to the morning service at St. Peter's. In a way it was consoling, and in a way it was sad. It was probably once a rich and vibrant church, but it had now fallen on bad times. There was a congregation of about twenty with a woman priest leading them in the liturgy. Probably twelve of them were gay man, with about three lesbians. The other five were straight, one a married couple. They didn't have a choir, but a small friendly looking woman was singing. She sounded like she might be an opera singer, but Colin wasn't sure. The service was over soon, and he joined the rag tag congregation down in the undercroft for coffee – what one of the more flamboyant gay men referred to as Holy Happy Hour.

"Hello, my name is Hildegarde," said the woman with the operatic voice that had lead the congregation in song, "Are you from this part of town?" She asked.

"My name is Colin. Actually, I'm visiting from Pittsburgh."

"Too bad, we could use more people in the congregation."

"Well, I wouldn't mind moving to Columbus, but my husband is a priest. I'm not sure if he would be happy here. What's the church like?"

"Officially not too gay friendly, but unofficially very gay support-ing. Nancy, come over here and meet a visitor from Pittsburgh."

"Hi, my name is Nancy," said the red haired woman. Colin could tell that she had a strong personality.

"Colin."

"You're from Pittsburgh?" She asked.

"Yes, just visiting for the weekend, although it looks like a nice enough place to live."

"Do you know a priest in Pittsburgh, Debbie Ranksullen?"

"No, actually I haven't been an Episcopalian too long, I was raised Catholic."

"Too bad for you," and without another word, she turned and walked away.

Taken a little aback, Colin endured the coffee hour, hoping that it would end soon. He made a mental note to keep the conversation Spartan here. He was always better at these things when Derek was around. Even though they often didn't spend the time talking together, or even attending as a couple, his presence made Colin feel a little more at ease. After playing ten thousand questions with the gay men, he excused himself. Then he had to go and retrieve a Billy that seemed to be besotted with the man that he met on Friday night. Finally, they left for Pittsburgh.

"I really don't want to go back Colin."

"I know Billy, except for Derek, neither do I."

"Do you think that I could find a job here?"

"I don't think that would be much of a problem. They seem to have many places for a young boy like you to work. I picked up a paper this morning, you can scan it for jobs—for both of us while he drive home."

Chapter 7

Once he was back in Pittsburgh, the regular routine made it seem that time was going by quickly. Colin and Derek's weekend getaway came and went too quickly as well. Their time together was good for the two of them and for their relationship. They came back to their regular lives, renewed and strengthened in their resolve to make it work. It wasn't that there was any major crisis in their life together, just a kind of monotony that placed a lethargic strain on the bond that they shared.

The first Saturday of April came with a gush of snow. While not typical, this was not unknown in Pittsburgh. It was the day that the cute Roman Catholic priest from down the street was coming to dinner at Colin and Derek's. The two had spent the morning in the strip district, planning a meal fit for a king. Actually the meal was as much for each of them as it was for the visitor. Gay men were always like this, preparing elaborate meals to assuage their own need for creativity.

The doorbell rang at 7:30 sharp, the time that Fr. Alphonse D'Amore was to arrive.

"Hello, I'm Colin, I don't think that we've met."

"Al D'Amore, a friend of Derek's"

"Hello Al, how are you?" Derek called out from the kitchen.

Soon the men were gathered around the living room fireplace, each with a strong drink in their hands. They planned on a late dinner, about eight thirty, so it was a leisurely time for them all to get to know each other a little better. The meal turned out to be a homosexual delight: a scallop and red pepper bisque, followed by a winter salad, then veal scallopini with pasta and Italian green beans. The dinner literally climaxed with a Fra'Angelico cheese-cake that Colin had made. It was served with coffee and brandy. As they were drinking their coffee, the conversation turned to things gay, and specifically to the Papal decoration for Brandon Mantune.

"I know, he's a sleaze, but what can I say, it wasn't my doing," Al replied to the questions that Colin had.

"I mean, I wouldn't mind and all, but one would think that the bar would be a little better for someone in the new Papal nobility. Don't they do background checks?" Colin continued.

"I don't know that much about it. We simple priests are often kept out of that high-class stuff. It's all done through the bishop's office. But it is an open joke, even among some of the monsignors."

"You've been to the bar?" Derek asked.

"Yes, I have, but not that often."

"You into leather, Al?" Colin asked, smiling into his brandy.

"Somewhat, basically a novice, no pun intended."

"Down boy," Derek said, smiling at his lover.

"Don't worry, I don't usually debauch the Catholic clergy."

"Just the Episcopal clergy?" Al asked joining in the little joke.

"They don't take vows of celibacy."

As soon as Colin said it, he knew that he had made a mistake. He hadn't intended an attack on Al's vocation, but he could see the pained look on the Italian priest's face.

"I'm sorry Al, sometimes I can be an ass," Colin said.

"No problem, actually the fault is mine. I have a hard time dealing with my commitment to my church and my sexuality. Some guys just lie, and some just become cranky celibates. I agonize over it."

"I shouldn't have brought it up, it was unthinking of me," Colin replied.

"Come on guys, we all know that it's not a perfect world. Let's just live in it, and leave the agony to those times when we feel the need for confession." Derek interceded, defusing this situation. "Let's get back to trashing Brandy."

"The last time that I was in that bar was in January, on a Thursday evening. Brandy was drunk and was all over that doctor that died. He told him that he could show him a good time," Al added, glad for the change in subject matter.

"Vlad was our friend," Derek interjected.

"I didn't know that Brandy was in any way interested in Vlad." Colin said with some surprise.

"Oh, come on. Brandy is interested in anything that walks," Derek replied, getting up to refill their coffees.

"Yeah, I know that he seems interested, it just all seems to phony to me. Like it's an act or something. I never take him seriously," Colin countered.

"I get the same feeling, and forgive the comparison, but it's like the priest after Mass, greeting the people and pretending to be genuinely interested in each and every one of them. Derek should know that feeling," Al said.

"I truly do care for each and every person I greet after Mass," Derek added, looking very smug, then bursting into laughter.

It was getting onto about eleven o'clock when the two priests decided that it was time that they call it a night. Colin was sorry for the evening to end, it was nice entertaining in their home, they did it so rarely, unless it was a church event. Al seemed like a really nice guy, somewhere between Derek and Colin's age. As he stopped at the door, he said, "Do you guys, ever.........um........have, like..... a.........."

Derek came to his aid, "A three-way?"

"Yes," Al replied, blushing.

"We sure do, and I would like it sometime. Colin, how about you? Feel like breaking another one of your taboos in the near future?" Derek asked putting his arm around Colin.

"With eyes like Al's, not to mention his almost perfect Italian brooding pout, I could do it. Don't worry Al, you're our friend now, we won't loose track of you."

After Al had left, and as they were walking up the stairs, Derek said, "I'm surprised at you, I didn't think that sex with an RC priest was a possibility, any time, any where."

"I learned a long time ago, my little prince, never say never."

The next morning, Colin couldn't help but noticing the slight wince in Derek's eyes whenever the choir started singing. Derek must have had too much to drink last night. The good priest looked a little hung over this morning, and the service dragged on, with the choir director adding his late Lenten dirges to give a sense drama to the service. Coffee hour looked particularly painful for Derek. Colin found Millicent and cornered her.

"Millicent, do you think you can run interference for Derek this morning. He's a little under the weather."

"Did you get carried away torturing him last night Colin?"

"No, just a protracted dinner that included a different liquor with each course."

"Are you two alcoholics, Colin?"

"Millicent, please put your claws back in. I know that life has dealt you a bad hand, but come on, don't attack us."

"You're right Colin," Millicent answered, looking truly remorseful. "I was taking my frustration about Michael out on you. By the way, I've decided to leave him. I hope that the parish will be supportive."

"I'm sure that they will, and positive that Derek will be. Is there anything that you need? Do you want to come over for dinner tonight?"

"No some things a girl has to do on her own. But please, once it's done, let me have some time with Derek without you getting all hot and bothered."

"It's a deal. And if there's anything that I can do, let me know."

Millicent went over, whispered in Derek's ear, and took over mid-stream in the conversation that he had been having with an octogenarian discussing a Princess Dianna garden for the spring.

"Thanks Colin, I need some rest," he said, barely loud enough for Colin to hear.

They walked back to the rectory and Colin put Derek to bed. His color didn't seem quite right. Colin was worried. What no one knew, except Colin and a few others was that Derek was HIV positive. He was healthy enough, the drugs had worked wonders on him, but, he tired quickly. He was responsible—telling his sexual partners before hand and always practicing safe sex, but Colin didn't think that they should make it public knowledge to his parishioners yet. True, he was positive when he arrived, positive long before he met Colin. But this was Pittsburgh, and he agreed with Colin that, perhaps the people should get used to a gay priest with a husband before the rest would be given to them.

Derek slept soundly. Colin, restless, and having drunk less than Derek the night before, went out to get a movie and some comfort food for his lover. He stopped by Border's and got Derek one more of those fantasy novels he was constantly reading and then went to the movie place and rented a couple of avant-garde gay movies that neither one of them had seen. He also rented *All About Eve*. Derek had to be one of the few gay men that Colin knew who hadn't seen the movie. The rest of the blustery afternoon and evening was spent with blankets, books, movies, cookies, and other earthly delights that Colin knew would help his lover recover. Or, if not recover, at least feel like a pampered child.

"Have you seen your doctor lately, Derek?" Colin asked during a break in the movie marathon.

"Yes. Please Colin, no lectures. I'm healthy, just can't carouse like I used to. Please don't get all over-protective again."

Their first year together had been fraught with discord because Colin felt that he had to monitor Derek's health. Actually, Derek's health was bad when they met   He had just started on protease inhibitors and was recovering from having less than 50 T-cells, suffering from multiple opportunistic infections over the course of his disease. Colin spent the first year driving him crazy with, did you take your pills, do you feel well, do you need a doctor. Finally, Derek gave Colin an ultimatum, one of the few times that he did, "If I needed a mother, I would have gone home." After that, Colin became a concerned, but hands-off lover. It worked much better that way. Colin had forgotten the first rule of gay spouses: you current lover does not want a parent or a mirage image of their last lover.

Derek started perking up late in the evening, just about the time Colin was thinking about calling it a day. Derek, who's day off was always Monday, didn't have the same need for an early night on Sundays.

"You feel like going to Starbuck's?" Derek asked.

"Well, look's like you've returned from the dead."

"I know that it's getting late, but I could use the company of a bunch of sexually ambitious college students. The only people that I saw today was the choir, and then a bunch of old Episcopalians."

"OK, we can go, I can stand to get out today anyway. But wear something warm, it's really cold out for April. Although, it's supposed to be 70 in a couple of days, but this is Pittsburgh."

Within a half an hour they found themselves cuddled around the fireplace at Starbuck's in Shadyside with a whole room full of graduate students studying. Colin brought a book and Derek was working on his Easter sermon over a cappuccino. It turned out to be a good idea, the company of so many people was consoling, even though it was snowing outside.

"Will it ever be spring?" Derek asked.

"All too soon, and then summer, and that blasted heat."

"It has been an exceptionally long winter this year, and it doesn't seem to be giving up at all."

"You're right about that. And it's hard to believe that it's been almost three months since Vlad's death."

"Nothing ever came of that. I was surprised that there wasn't a major investigation and the usual media hype about ritual death and all of that."

"Well, the hospital had a lot to do with keeping it out of the media. Then there was the fact that he was a foreign national and the body had to be shipped back to his family. Funny, I don't know one thing about his family."

"And I was supposed to plan a memorial. As soon as Easter is over, I'm doing it. It will be the biggest memorial since the Matthew Shepard thing that we did."

"Wasn't Fr. Al's comment a little scary last night. Brandy and Vlad. That's absolutely amazing."

"Yeah, and the feelings that we have that Brandy is phony, like he's pretending to be turned on by all of us. Oh, and, by the way, you might want to drop the Father with Al, especially if we're ever going to play together. It just doesn't sound right, Come on Father, get down there and lick those boots clean."

"I'm still struggling with that one. But this whole Brandy and Vlad thing has me concerned. Do you remember that gay podiatrist from some bum-fuck place outside the city, found the same way a few months before?"

"Vaguely, but I've forgotten it now."

"He was found by his brother when they couldn't reach him. He was handcuffed with a rope around his neck, dead."

"I had forgotten about that. You're right. Do you suppose that there might be some sort of connection?"

"Maybe, but we'll probably never know."

"You're right. Hey, we should go. You have to go to your work-a-day world tomorrow morning. What's on the agenda at the hospital?"

"Oh, the usual, people being fired for being ten minutes late, budgets not being approved, physicians angry about the state of supplies, and patient's families upset at the care that their loved ones are receiving. The usual. Once it was fun, now it's just a job. And not a very pleasant one at that. I really don't like some of those people. We choose supervisors and administration in hospitals all the wrong way.

If you're a good nurse or lab tech, you're made a supervisor, without any of the requisite skills. Once in those positions, the people tend to think that they have it made, and no longer need to exert any effort on the part of their jobs."

"Why don't you just chuck it all in and quit?"

"Would you be willing to support me?"

"For a while, you know that we've made that commitment. But the question becomes, could you simply be the Rector's wife?"

"Ask me that tomorrow morning about nine. Usually by that time I'm in the thick of it."

They gathered their belongings and, as they got up to leave, two graduate students jumped in their chairs. Laughing as they left the coffee shop, Colin and Derek made their way back to their house as winter left its final mark on the city. It had been a good weekend, and both men were satisfied. It was just the right mix of people and solitude. While it couldn't be done every week, Derek's liver would never stand the strain, it was pleasant when it happened. Colin hoped that it would happen more often while he was picturing himself as the Rector's spouse, heading up the women's auxiliary and the altar guild—maybe the tense atmosphere of the hospital wasn't all that bad after all. Derek couldn't be consulted, he had already fallen asleep, so Colin wrapped him in his arms and cuddled under the warm of the quilt. In a short time, he was also asleep.

Chapter 8

Easter came and went with it's usual display of religious fervor and excitement. The delayed memorial service for Vlad was held with Colin providing the eulogy. He knew Vlad more than any of the others, but it was hard for him to make this formal goodbye. Funny, without the stark reality of the dead body, and without the comfort of a funeral, Colin, along with many of the others, didn't quite believe in their hearts that Vlad was dead. Now it all seemed so real. Derek knew the usefulness of the funeral service, a time to say good bye and a time to confront the reality of the person's death. Colin discovered this all on his own, and, after the service, the friends began their grieving. This time the emotions were true grief, not the disbelief that held them in awe last January in Washington.

At the reception after the service, everyone sat around extolling the virtues of Vlad while lamenting his loss. Everyone that is, except Brandon Mantune, Knight of His Holiness.

"Well Dirk, I guess that you were the last one to see that dick of his in action." Brandy exclaimed, a little too loudly.

"I didn't really get to see it in action that night. We both lost interest when we got to his house."

"You mean he lost interest in you," the loud mouthed bar owner replied.

"Gentlemen, a little more respect here," Colin interjected, trying to get Dirk out of what had to be an uncomfortable spot. Colin knew that Dirk was filled with anxiety over going home with Vlad that night, and was embarrassed about the rejections of his sexual advances. When Dirk became Mr. Steel City Leather, Brandy was his best friend and promoter. When Dirk did not win as the regional contest and was not subsequently sent on to Mr. World or whatever, Brandy no longer had any use for him. That's what Colin disliked most about this man, not only his façade of being the friendly bar owner, but his total disloyalty to those who no longer help him in his obsession with becoming the leather bar owner of the world.

The quick curt comment by Colin managed to put Brandy in his place, and he skulked off to a corner. Billy was there also, with the new man that he had found in Columbus. The two were in negotiations now about where they would live, and, if Billy moved to Columbus, what he would do to make a living. Millicent was there, without her cranky husband, and even good Fr. Alphonse from down the street attended, vested, and offered a prayer for their slain comrade.

Without the center of attention being directed at him, Brandy looked forlorn, and almost sad. Derek, ever the priest, went over and tried to involve him in a conversation, or at least draw him into the conversations of others. Funny, they never taught this in the seminary, but it was one of the most important lessons for a priest to learn.

"Father. . . . I just can't get used to calling you that. . . . I need to talk to you," Brandy whispered with a voice harassed by too many cigarettes and too much booze.

"Please, just call me Derek. What can I do for you?"

"I think I would like to go to confession."

Now, while it is true that Episcopalians do go to confession, and while Anglo-Catholic Episcopalians do so with great abandon and ceremony, it simply isn't done all that often in the normal routine of the Episcopalian priest. Especially not to hear the confession of a Catholic.

"Brandy, Fr. Alphonse is here, it might be more appropriate for you to approach him, he's part of your faith community."

"I don't want Fr. Alphonse, I want you."

"But, by participating in this sacramental rite with me, you are separating yourself from the Roman Church, not by anything the Episcopal church says, but by the rules of the Roman Church."

"Derek, I said that I want you to hear my confession. Now, will you do it or not?"

"Of course I will, when would you like for me to do this," Derek replied with a sigh that said he was capitulating, but that he didn't agree with what he was doing.

"Right now."

"Would you like to wait until everyone leaves?"

"No, right now."

Derek told him to go and wait in his office, while he went about saying a few words to a couple of the people at the reception. He told Colin to take over for him, that he had a errand to complete. Colin, while looking a little perplexed, agreed and his lover left the room, hoping that Brandy found his office without too much trouble.

When he entered, he found Brandy sitting nervously in front of his desk. Derek sat down on the other side, opened a drawer and pulled out a purple stole, putting it around his neck and looking at Brandy.

"Bless me, for I have sinned."

"The Lord be in your heart and upon your lips that you may truly and humbly confess your sins: In the Name of the Father, and of the Son, and of the Holy Spirit. Amen," Derek began the ritual, tracing the sign of the cross over Brandy's head.

"I don't know where to begin. This is really the only time that I have ever been to confession. You see, I'm not a Catholic, I was born and raised in the Episcopal church, and, around where I come from, we don't do this all that often.

Derek, hiding his surprise that the man that so recently accepted a Papal honor from the Roman Church was not Catholic, answered him, "Brandy, all you have to do is tell me the sinful things that you remember in your life. My first question is, why, to all the world, do you appear to be a Roman Catholic."

"Well, it is Pittsburgh, and the norm here is Catholic. I just started going to one of the churches and registered, that's all. I kept going and that's the end of it. I go to Mass and communion every Sunday."

"The Roman Catholic church would say that you are committing a sacrilege by receiving communion without the proper preparation. But I'm way out of my league on this one."

"Anyway, what really brings me here today is not that at all. I don't have any problems with that. First thing, I sometimes have sex with men."

Derek, looking even more confused than with the Catholic-Episcopal thing, added, "Brandy, you own a gay bar, and, in this humble priest's opinion, having sex with men isn't a matter of sin."

"But you see Father, it *is* a matter of sin. It is so wrong for one man to have sexual relations with another. The Bible says that it's an abomination before the Lord."

"Brandy, while we can possibly deal with this issue right now in confession, perhaps you would like to see a counselor. You have some fairly serious issues that you need to deal with, and not only on a spiritual level."

"I want to be free of this guilt."

"But you own a gay bar! If you think this is wrong, isn't it wrong to provide a place for others to participate in this sin?" Derek couldn't believe that he was taking this tact in the conversation. He straightened his stole, and resolved to let this man unburden his soul.

"I've had sex with men about three or four times. Only within the last couple of years. It's really bothering me."

"I understand, is there anything else?"

"Yes, twice I couldn't stand it. . . . having sex with them. . . . and I hurt them."

"When you say that you hurt them, did you cause them some significant pain, or beat them up, or what?"

"I made them hang themselves with the rope that we were using in a bondage scene."

Derek's blood froze right there. He stared into the other man's eyes, wondering, for one brief moment if this were some sort of sick joke that Brandy was playing on him. After the momentary initial shock, he felt his heart rend in two. For the only time in his life, his commitment to the gay community and his commitment to the church came into conflict for him. As a priest, he was bound by rules that required him to maintain the secrecy of this act, and yet, he was incensed that a man could commit such atrocities, simply because he couldn't get over the guilt of his own desires.

"Was Vlad one of these people?"

"Yes."

Derek could feel the noose tightening around his own chest. He wanted to reach out and hit Brandy across the face. He wanted to run out of the room and get someone from the police to arrest him. He wanted to run back into the other room were Vlad's friends were and yell that it was Brandy that did it. In his anger, he stared at the cross on the wall opposite his desk, feeling the same kind of abandonment that Christ must have felt when he was nailed to its wood.

"Brandy, there are a couple of things that you must do right away. You need to find someone to deal with these issues with you in a counseling situation. You also need to go to the authorities and tell them what you have done."

"No, I can't do it. I have kids, and I don't want them to know about this."

"But I thought that you were this major leather person who started a bar where like minded people could go."

"I started a bar so I could make money. I saw what was lacking and went ahead and did it. Around all those guys, I just started to think that I would like to get a little of the action, if you know what I mean."

"Like I said, you must....."

"It simply isn't going to happen, Father. I'm not going to confess to anyone but you."

"How do you know that I wouldn't go to the authorities?"

"Aren't there rules about this, and besides, what proof do you have, it will be my word against yours."

Derek then realized the full impact of what had just happened to him. He knew, from this moment on, that he would never be the same. The sin of the man before him had somehow entered into his own life and destroyed it. He didn't know how he would ever function again. Life became drained of vitality. He had entered into a conversation with evil itself, and he would not come out unscathed.

"That's it. Those are my sins."

Derek didn't know what to do next. Obviously, the man sitting in front of him had never read the Book of Common Prayer, so he didn't know what was to be done next either. Normally Derek would pronounce the words of absolution and the rite would be ended. He didn't want to. He found himself hating this man. Never in his life was it so hard for him to do anything. With trembling hands and a quiver in his voice he waved the absolution over Brandy's head, assuming that it was not his choice to withhold God's pardon. Brandy got up and left the office. It was then Derek realized that during the past couple of minutes, he himself, had become nailed to the cross on the wall across from his desk.

He went back out into the hall. They must have been in there for quite some time, since no one was left at the reception. He walked into the church. He knelt down in front of the altar, buried his head in his hands, and wept like a child.

A Boner Book

Chapter 9

The days and weeks after that fateful moment seemed, in some ways, to pass quickly, while at the same time, to stand still. Derek had managed to salvage some composure and continued on in the land of the living. He and Colin had both been busy during those fateful weeks. Summer was beginning, and while that day had not slipped from his consciousness, Derek managed to deal with it. Colin had noticed that since the memorial for Vlad that Derek had become a little quieter and withdrawn. He attributed it to a delayed sense of grief. He gave his lover a lot of leeway during this time.

They hadn't been out in quite a while, and their sex life was almost nil. When there was sex it was kind of perfunctory, and nothing major, certainly nothing that would take place in the basement. One Friday morning, Colin decided to try and pull his lover out of whatever mood that he was in.

"What do you say to getting dressed up in leather and having a night on the town?"

"Where would we go?" Was the only answer that Derek could give.

"Well, if we're in leather, we should probably limit it to the bar."

"I never want to go to that bar again."

Colin didn't press. He knew the tone in Derek's voice that said back off, the issue is closed. He was at a total loss; he didn't know what to do. He wasn't sure if he had done something wrong, if Derek was mad about something or what. It couldn't be Billy, he hadn't seen him in a long time, now that the boy was enthralled with the body builder from Columbus.

"Are you feeling all right?" Colin asked.

"Yeah, I feel OK. I just don't want to go to that bar again. It gives me the creeps. I don't know what it is. You can go out if you want or need to."

"No, that's ok. How about a movie?"

"Well, I'll go to a movie with you if you take me to dinner first."

"It's a date, you pick the movie."

Colin went to work that day feeling out of sorts. He just didn't understand what his lover was feeling. He wanted to help, but knew that he couldn't press any further. The day at the hospital was filled with the usual busy work that kept administrators' work-a-day world occupied.

"Mr. Morgan? May I see you about the budget?" The somewhat disheveled laboratory supervisor said as she poked her head into the room.

"Sure, Betty, what's up?"

"My budget has been cut again, and I have to eliminate another position. I can't do it."

"Betty, I understand, but the board has let us know that there just isn't a great deal of money to be had."

"Everyone is working at 110%. We can't keep this up for long."

Colin couldn't believe that with everything happening to him, he had to deal with these petty problems. He didn't set the budget, merely oversaw its development. He knew this woman well, and, in his opinion, she shouldn't be in her position. She had no imagination, and, he suspected that she didn't give her 110%, only saw to it that her employees gave theirs.

"Well Betty, maybe you could find some new way of doing things. New equipment, consolidation, or something."

"Nope. We're cut to the very bone. There's nothing more to give."

"Well, if that's the case, we may have to see about contracting our laboratory services from an outside source."

That stopped the woman dead in her tracks. Colin used this technique often. He really wasn't considering contracting out the services, but he knew that if he suggested it, she would be forced to consider new ways of doing things. He really wasn't proposing that she eliminate an employee that had a job, just give up an unfilled position. He took special delight in seeing the look of horror on her face.

"Well, maybe there's something that we can do," was her reply after she took a minute to regain her composure."

"I thought that might be the case. See my assistant. Set up a meeting with you and the other supervisor, your administrative and medical directors for Tuesday. We'll go through our options."

"Thanks for your time," she said, clearly not happy with Colin's response.

He was glad when she was gone. He really didn't like her, but he had to be nice to her. He hated using that intimidation technique, but he was known for it throughout the hospital. It made him a more efficient administrator, and often forced a reluctant underling to come up with a solution that was there all the time, but a solution that just needed to be fleshed out a little.

The rest of the day was spent putting out these little fires. The executive staff, those vice-presidents that dealt with the business end of the hospital, liked him for doing these little jobs himself, instead of appointing a host of others to do that for him. It also meant that they came to him with every minor complaint that managed to make it up the administrative ladder. It was, however, his job to do these things, and he did them rather well.

He checked the paper before leaving work to find a movie that Derek would like to see. He had already made reservations at the expensive French restaurant in Shadyside that Derek loved. They had been there only twice before in the years that they lived in Friendship, the bordering neighborhood. Each time it cost them over a hundred dollars for dinner for two, but Colin thought that Derek needed a little coddling. He had been in such a mood lately.

As he was getting ready to leave, the phone rang.

"Hi Colin, what's up?"

"Billy, one of your few days in Pittsburgh? Or is Mr. Wonderful coming to your city this weekend."

"I'm not sure, he's being kind of weird."

"Oh Billy, these things happen. We men can be difficult creatures to understand. Gay relationships are not that easy to start," all the while he was thinking that they weren't that easy to continue or to end for that matter, but he didn't want to project his jaded view onto such a young boy.

"I know. I was wondering if you have any time for me this evening."

As much as he wanted and needed the sex that Billy was, in his round about way, proposing, he couldn't. "No Billy, sorry, I've promised this evening to Derek. He's been kind of out of it lately, and I thought that a real life date would do him some good." Colin said, making a mental note to kick himself later, passing up such a good time.

"I understand, hope that the date works. Give me a call next week sometime, OK?"

"Sure will."

Colin got home that evening to find Derek in conference with Millicent. She had made the final decision about her divorce and they were working out the details of how it would or should be revealed to the congregation. He guessed that these things weren't that easy for a woman priest. After all, they are supposed to be models of Christian living. It must be hard for them when their lives fall apart right in front of an ever-vigilant congregation.

Derek and Millicent finished quickly after they heard Colin coming in. She left the rectory. Before Derek went to find Colin, he picked up the phone and dialed Fr. Alphonse down the street.

"Hey Al, how are you doing?"

"Fine, and you, Derek?"

"Hanging in there, but I have a question. Have you ever heard anything in confession that really bothered you?"

"A thousand times. Someone's beating their wife, someone is molesting their children, alcoholism, theft, you name it."

"What do you do when you feel that your continued silence outside the confessional is wrong?"

"I stay silent. Period. There aren't any options for me. Why do you ask?"

"Oh, I heard a confession a while ago, and it seems to keep on bothering me."

"One of my seminary professors told me that I should pray to forget what I heard in the confessional, otherwise it might drive me crazy."

"Wise man. Good advice."

"Really Derek, if you need to talk, I can talk with you about it sometime, and I don't mean for you to reveal what you know."

"Thanks Al, I might take you up on it."

"How's Colin?"

"He's doing OK, but I've been a little preoccupied lately, so he's probably feeling a little wounded."

"Well, if you are aware of the problem, make it up to him. You guys have a great relationship, and they aren't that easy to find these days."

"Thanks Al." Derek hung up the phone, and immediately picked it up again. Consulting his schedule, he made reservations for a hotel room in Washington in a few weeks. He would surprise Colin with the news that they were going out of town for a weekend. That would cheer his lover up. It might help his mood as well.

The evening was perfect. The food was good, the waiter was cute, and the movie that Colin had picked was wonderful. They got home that evening and made love like they hadn't in quite some time. True, they didn't go to the basement, but there was a lot of emotion and a lot of passion from both men as they came together for the first time in days.

"We need a dog," Derek proclaimed as he finished getting a late night snack after their lovemaking was over.

"That's the last thing that we need, we aren't even responsible enough for ourselves."

"Come on Colin, let's get a dog."

"And who is going to take care of it?"

"I will."

"Yeah right, don't make me be the daddy in this thing."

"OK, we both will."

"And when we go away?" Colin asked, using the trump card of tying them down to a responsibility that would limit their ability to travel.

"Millicent would watch the dog. It would be good for her."

"You're probably right about that one, but can we put this on the back burner for a little while?"

"When you put things on the back burner, they tend not to be dealt with, ever."

"I promise you, when summer is over, we'll come back to this."

"OK."

"Colin?"

"Yes?"

"I love you."

"I love you too. Thanks for letting me know."

"Can I have a dog?"

"Bitch!"

"I don't care—it could be male or female."

" I was ...." But before Colin could finish they both started laughing. It was the first time that they had laughed together like that in a while. Things were starting to get back on the right track. Colin fell asleep that night happy that whatever had affected their relationship during these past few weeks no longer seemed to matter. He wondered what it was that had such an effect on Derek, but didn't feel the need to dwell on it for long. Right now he was just happy that things were getting back to normal.

Derek felt a relief as well. Yes, the problem was still there, but life would go on. It was good to fall asleep with a man you just had sex with, especially after the date like the one that they had tonight. It was good to have a date with your lover sometimes. It renews interest. Maybe it would keep Colin from longing for Billy. Derek wasn't really jealous. He just knew that Colin and Billy had a special something going on there. It didn't threaten him. Colin would never leave him for Billy, it just wasn't his style. Besides, he just knew that they would be getting a dog soon.

Chapter 10

The Washington trip came up quickly, and was quite a surprise for Colin. Derek had checked with Colin's assistant to insure that he could go. That Friday, when he looked at his schedule and Martin told him that he was in a meeting all afternoon, he seemed a little confused. He didn't remember scheduling the meeting and Martin was being evasive about what it concerned. Derek called and asked if they could meet for an early lunch. When Colin agreed, he told him to be at the side entrance of the hospital at eleven thirty, and he would pick him up. Derek had already packed their bags and put them in the trunk. He picked up Colin at eleven thirty sharp.

Colin wasn't paying too much attention as Derek pulled onto the parkway and headed for the turnpike. It wasn't until they were passing the Wilkinsburg exit that he said:

"Hey, we can't go too far, I have some kind of meeting this afternoon from one until four. Where are you planning to take us for lunch?"

"Anna Marie's," Derek answered, naming an Italian restaurant on Connecticut Avenue, just north of Dupont Circle.

"Yeah, right."

"Actually, that's where we're going. And before you start in with your excuses and attentions to detail, Martin knows about it. Your schedule has been cleared, and everything is packed in the trunk. We will be back Sunday night."

"What brought all this on?" Colin asked as he turned, smiled at his lover, and grabbed his knee.

"You've had it pretty rough lately with me, I thought that you might need a little get-away weekend. I know how you love them."

"Care to talk about what's been bothering you?"

"I really can't. I can just tell you that it has nothing to do with us."

"We're OK?"

"We're definitely OK."

Within a few hours, they were strolling around Dupont Circle. They always seemed happiest here. They were both familiar with many cities, most gay men were these days. But it was the quiet atmosphere of Dupont Circle that they liked most of all. It was cosmopolitan, and certainly filled with gay men, but wasn't the rat race of Manhattan or the overkill of San Francisco.

The two days were filled with coffee shops, bookstores, and wonderful lunches. The nights had them donning their finest leather apparel and making the rounds of the bars.

"How come we don't go out in Pittsburgh any more?" Colin asked his lover over a drink and a unusually quiet moment in one of the leather bars.

"I've had some problems, Colin. I plan on facing them when we get back. I know it hasn't been fair to you, and that we haven't seen many of our bar friends, but, don't worry, when we get back, we can start going again."

"You certainly are filled with mystery. Have you been having an affair on me?"

"Most certainly, not."

Sunday they went to the Liturgy at the National Cathedral. It was often hard for Colin to get used to his lover at his side in church, he was so accustomed to seeing him at the altar. It was a good feeling for both of them. It was when they were in the pews together that he felt like they had gone to church together. It made no sense, but that's how Colin felt. A leisurely lunch in Chevy Chase was followed by an equally leisurely ride home. Sunday evening found them in bed waiting for the next installment of *Sex in the City*. They both marveled at how this HBO comedy about four Manhattan women had become a gay obsession.

Derek felt good, better than he had been in weeks. The weekend was a success. He had managed to prove to Colin that their relationship was still strong. Colin even looked more rested now as well. Derek was, however feeling unusually tired. Perhaps it was from the late nights in DC, but he made a mental note to see his physician, just to be on the safe side.. It had been a while, and maybe he just needed a little check up. He also made a note to schedule Colin's annual exam. His lover tended to neglect his medical responsibilities, most hospital people did. Looking out for him made Derek feel completely domestic. The only thing that was missing was a faithful dog, curled up at their feet or on the floor beside the bed. He would keep Colin to his promise, when the summer was ending, they would get a dog. Then, the only thing left would be to bring up the discussions about their place of abode. They really had to get out of Pittsburgh soon—there simply was no gay life here. The bars tended to suck and most of them were in very bad neighborhoods. Speaking of which, Derek made one final mental note: they would definitely be at the *Pirate's Nest* this weekend.

The next Friday night, Derek suggested that they go out. He was busy with a church meeting until nine. He told Colin that he would rush upstairs and change. They were going to the bar. Colin was shocked at this seemingly sudden change in Derek. He just continued to be happy that whatever was wrong before had somehow been fixed. Derek was apprehensive, he didn't know how he would react to Brandy, or, for that matter, how Brandy would react to him.

They walked into the bar and were greeted by Brandy's ever present, "Hello dudes, it's about time that I see you in here again."

Colin and Derek both thought that someone over the age of forty-five, maybe even fifty, should drop the word 'dude' from their vocabulary. Derek was a little surprised that Brandy showed no anxiety whatsoever at being confronted for the first time with the man that he had confessed a murder to.

They both mumbled something about we've been busy, nice to see you, and went further into the dimly lit bar.

Colin was amazed that while it had been a few months since they had been in the bar, the picture was still the same. The same faces, dressed in the same leather, all standing around, almost in the same positions. He knew at that point that Pittsburgh was indeed a small town.

Colin bought them drinks and started chatting with Dirk.

"Hey Dirk, sorry about the leather contest."

"No problem, I was actually relieved not to win. You can't imagine the pressure that you are under when you are a title holder."

Derek intervened before the last comment could send Colin into a rage about the whole leather contest mentality that was invading the practice of leather and S/M as he knew it. "Dirk, it's not very busy here for a Friday, what's up?"

"Oh, the boy speaks. Sir, may I speak to your boy?" Dirk asked Colin.

Colin was mildly amused and somewhat pleased that he heard the old guard etiquette being practiced.

"Of course Dirk, you know that you always have permission, and that he has permission to speak to you."

Colin and Derek had originally followed some of those old rules when they first met. At that time, Derek thought that he wanted to be a total slave to the man that he called his master. Over the years, actually over the first few months, they both knew that those rules simply couldn't be followed in the extreme. Perhaps when masters and slaves were simply that, they could work. When the Master fell in love with the slave, it was a whole different ball game. Now, most of those old rules only came out when Colin had a bug up his ass about something, or when Derek knew that he had really overstepped his boundaries, and was trying to make up. As Dirk and Derek were talking, Colin kept wondering whether those strict regulations were followed anywhere. He was the first to complain when he ran into a group of men dressed in leather only as a fashion statement. However, he was also the first to say that the practice of leather has to change with the time and the circumstances. Ultimately, it was the decision of the men involved with the relationship, and their degree of comfort.

"Hey Colin, how are you and Derek doing?" Todd asked as he approached the men.

"We're just fine," replied Colin.

"Where have you both been? No one has seen you."

"Well, we've both been busy, and besides, sometimes we have to take a break from the bar."

"I thought maybe you guys were in hiding after Vlad's unfortunate accident."

Derek could feel that noose again, tightening in his chest. Would he never be able to forget about that murder? "Todd, no we're not. And I'm not so sure that it was an accident, but let's try to forget it. Vlad was our friend, and we miss him dearly."

"Sorry, I didn't mean to. . . "

"That's OK, I didn't mean to snap at you. It's still a little fresh in my mind, that's all," Derek said as he tried to recover his composure.

The rest of the evening was spent standing around like a Royal couple, accepting the well wishes and minor gossip of the same group of men that they had seen for years in this bar: Mark, Dave, Dirk, Chuck, three Lees, two Michaels, and one Bruce thrown in for good measure. At one point, late in the night, Billy and his body builder from Columbus came into the bar. Colin was glad that the two had managed to settle whatever differences they had been having a while back.

When they had been there a legitimate amount of time, Colin was relieved when Derek finally gave him that special look that said it was time to go home. They said their good-byes and happily got into their car and drove home. They talked a little about the bar, and a lot about the upcoming visit of the bishop to Derek's parish for confirmation. Derek was a little anxious about it, and shared his concerns with his lover. Colin was unusually empathetic, abandoning his usual sarcasm about Derek's inability to get along with the man. Derek just had been too vulnerable lately.

Chapter 11

The day for the bishop's visit to St. Swithen's arrived all too soon for Derek, and for Millicent, as well. She would have to tell her boss that she had begun the divorce proceedings. She felt that he would not be very sympathetic to her cause in this matter. The choir was practicing early that morning for the ten thirty service. The bishop would arrive at eight for breakfast and a meeting with the clergy. The celebration of the liturgy and confirmation would be at ten thirty, followed by a reception/brunch instead of the usual coffee hour.

Derek clenched his teeth as the bishop's car pulled up. Mercifully, he was alone. He must have left his wife at home, or she simply had enough of church. He also didn't have any priest assistants with him—that too was good, at least he wouldn't be showing off in front of them.

"Good morning, bishop," Derek said in his church door voice, walking out to greet the man that he had to pretend to like for the day.

"Good morning Father, it looks like we will have a nice day."

"Millicent and I have been praying for that."

"Oh good, I am always edified when I hear that the clergy are praying. With all the changes in our church I wonder sometimes if that went out as well."

As they walked back into the church hall, where the breakfast for the trio was being served, the bishop saw Millicent. "Good morning Mother Millicent, how are you today?"

Millicent absolutely hated being called Mother Millicent. She couldn't believe that this unusual title was still used, she thought that it would have died a quick and merciful death. Actually, she couldn't ever believe that it had ever been placed into use, since female clergy in the Episcopal church hadn't been around all that long, and the title seemed to come from some bygone age.

"Good Morning bishop, how are you?" She replied cheerfully.

"I'm doing OK, and looking forward to meeting the parish today."

What neither Millicent or Derek had the heart to tell the man, was that the parish was not looking forward to meeting him. They both fought hard to convince the vestry not to call in an outside bishop for the confirmation. The parish simply didn't like the bishop's politics or his theology. Some of the older women, true Episcopalians, didn't like the way he conducted services. It wasn't that they minded the High Church routine, although they could really do away with it, it was that the bishop didn't do it very well.

The breakfast was progressing well, with the two priests bringing the bishop up to date on the state of the parish. While these visits weren't really inspections, the bishop often would judge how things were going during them. As they were lingering over coffee, Millicent broached the difficult subject of her divorce.

"Bishop, I do have some bad news. My marriage is failing, it simply isn't working anymore. Michael and I have decided to divorce."

She expected something from her spiritual mentor. Anything except the silence and the hard stare that she received from the bishop. It was several minutes before the elder cleric replied.

"This is very serious, Mother. Are you sure that you have tried everything that can be done without taking such a drastic step."

"Yes bishop, I have."

Derek decided to act as advocate. "You see Bishop, Millicent has been very unhappy for some time."

Before he could continue his train of thought, he was cut off by the bishop, "Father Derek, I do not need you to explain the situation. The last time that I checked, unhappiness was not grounds for simply ending a vow to God. We can't have our clergy jumping from bed to bed, no matter what the last general convention tried to pass."

As Derek was about to enter into an outright argument with the bishop, Millicent jumped to her own defense, "Bishop, that's simply not fair. I haven't been jumping from bed to bed, I have been with the same man, the only man that I have ever been with, for some time now. I have tried to make it work. He simply causes me a great deal of unhappiness. Not that it is any of your business but the man abuses me. Not physically, or I wouldn't have stayed this long, but mentally."

"Mother, I am sorry. I didn't mean to imply that your morals were lax. I was simply trying to demonstrate the enormity of what you are doing. Have you gone to the parish with this?"

"What do you mean, have I gone to the parish! Does the parish live with that man? No! Does he constantly put down the parish? No! I don't think that they have a lot to do with it!"

"They deserve to know."

"And they will know. I didn't want to tell them yet. I wanted to tell you first."

"They may no longer want you here then."

Derek could hold his tongue no longer. "I seriously doubt that bishop. The parish is very supportive, and we, as a church, and now I'm including you, don't ask people to stay in relationships that are damaging. The whole purpose of marriage is the building up of the two people."

"Father, I will not be lectured by you on the theology of marriage. You, of all people, cannot do that. Your lifestyle may have a different view of marriage that the rest of the world, however, how dare you exclude the siring of children from one of the true ends of marriage."

For one minute, Derek considered getting into the theological battle. To him, marriage was all about the two people. Children, to use the antiquated scholastic term the bishop seems so fond of holding onto was merely an accident of the sacrament—something that happened that was not essential to the sacrament. If the bishop held that children were the end of, and the reason for, marriage, he would have a hard time explaining to childless couples the situation in which they found themselves

The time was getting late, and both Derek and Millicent were thankful for that. "Bishop, I think we should adjourn, clear our heads, and prepare for the Eucharist," Derek said, hoping for a few quiet moments before he had to enter into the most sacred of mysteries of his church.

"That's a very good idea Father."

The bishop went to take a walk in the garden that separated the church from the rectory. The two priests went into the sacristy to make sure that all was prepared. The choir was milling about in various corners, and the organist was running around as if he had just been told that the world was ending in five minutes. Millicent finally went downstairs to spend a few minutes with the confirmation class and their teacher before the ceremony.

Just when Derek was about to get mad all over again, Colin popped into the sacristy, "How's it going?"

"He's a tired old man who has lost track of his church," the priest said in a stage whisper.

"Calm down, little one. It's only a few hours more, and then you're done with him here for another year."

"I can't stand it anymore."

"I know."

"No, you don't! You wouldn't work in a situation like this, and yet, you expect me to."

"I'm sorry Derek, I really am. But getting mad at me isn't going to do any good today."

Colin squeezed his lover's shoulder and left, taking a seat in the congregation. Now Derek felt like crap. He managed to fight, not only with a bishop this morning, but his lover as well. He couldn't believe how badly this day was turning out. Just at that minute, the bishop entered the sacristy and started to get vested for the liturgy. Derek introduced him to the altar servers and the various ministers for the ceremony. Millicent entered, and with that whipped dog look that Derek had seen so often, began to get vested herself.

The actual liturgy went well, the music was nice, the altar servers knew the routine, and the bishop didn't fumble too much through the liturgy. Even the bishop's sermon was bearable. Derek was wishing that the reception/brunch would go as smoothly. He really was hoping that it would be over, and that this awful man would be out of his space again.

The food at the brunch was great. The women, and a lot of the gay men, had done well. People were all being personable and Derek had managed to get cornered by an old woman lamenting the loss of the 1928 prayer book. As he was trying to console her, he looked across the room. Only one of his parishioners was talking to the bishop—Colin.

Amazing, the very man that disliked him so much because he was married to a man could only find one person to talk with him, his spouse.

"Well bishop, I would say that was a nice service this morning," Colin said using his best administrative 'I'm-your-friend' voice.

"Yes, and a nice day it was."

"It's a great parish, bishop. And, without being even a little prejudiced, the clergy here are great as well."

"Well, I'll have to take that one with a grain of salt. I don't imagine that you are very objective in that assessment."

Colin could see that he had made the bishop a little uncomfortable. Usually he reveled in that, but today, for some reason, it just seemed unkind. "I'm sorry bishop, I've made you uncomfortable."

"Think nothing of it. I struggle with what I know is right and trying to be a kind man."

"One question, and please don't take this the wrong way. Have you ever considered that being gay wasn't all that bad in the eyes of the Lord?"

"I don't think that's even a possibility. You have the scripture telling us that it is wrong."

"We both know that there are many ways to interpret scripture, and the texts aren't as clear as they are made to seem. I have always thought that the words of Christ were sufficient in determining a good sense of what was right and what was wrong."

"It's the whole book Colin, not just a part of it. And, the words of Christ are specific about sexual impropriety. Think of the woman caught in adultery."

"But Christ didn't condemn her."

"He told her to go and sin no more."

"Perhaps he was telling her that her sin wasn't really a sin. Perhaps he was absolving her from guilt," and Colin began laughing, knowing that he had reached an absurdity in his argument.

"I would take it from that laugh, that you have learned the error of your ways," the bishop continued, smirking.

"Just the absurdity of my argument at that moment. Christ only condemned the mean-spirited in the Gospels. He left all others relatively alone."

"We aren't going to agree on this one, Colin. You know that."

"I know, but I just don't understand why the homosexual issue has become a test for orthodoxy in the church. Not only a test, but *the* test. It's like, OK, you're a Christian, what do you think of homosexuality? If you answer it's just an alternative lifestyle, you're condemned. If you say, well, I don't see the problem, I'm gay myself, you're beyond condemned."

"Aren't you being a little mean-spirited in that case?" The bishop responded, clearly uncomfortable with the conversation.

"Perhaps, but I don't think so. However, I do know one thing, I am monopolizing your time, and you need to be available to the rest of the parish. They don't see you all that often."

"Perhaps you're right Colin."

Neither one of the men knew if they were being cut off by the other or not. Colin snaked his way through the room and found his lover. He came just in time to rescue him from a gay man who was going on about his latest trip to NYC and the liturgy at St. Mary the Virgin in Manhattan. When Colin got near, Derek politely excused himself.

"What were you and His Grace in such a deep conversation about?" Derek asked his lover.

"Actually, our theological differences concerning homosexuality."

"Yeah right, what were you really talking about?"

"I was being serious, Derek."

"You're kidding. Did you two come to any sort of agreement?"

"No, let's just say that we've entered into the cold war stage of the bishop-gay priest's spouse relationship."

"Well, don't feel bad. He read Millicent the riot act this morning, and managed to put me down at the same time."

"I really am sorry, Derek."

"OK, but just to warn you. After you get me that puppy, we are seriously going to sit down and have a talk about where we are living. This environment is just too oppressive for me. Not to mention stressful."

"If one of us had a job anywhere—I would go along. I can be poor but happy."

"I don't want to be poor."

"Now, now, my good priest. Doesn't that seem a little materialistic?"

"I'm an Episcopalian, not a Franciscan!"

As they started laughing, the two men turned to scan the crowd. There, in the corner, stood the bishop. Not one single parishioner was talking to him. He looked so alone. Colin said that he should go and rescue him, Derek said no—let him stand in his regal solitary splendor. After a painful several minutes, finally, it was Millicent who went to engage the bishop in conversation, saving him the embarrassment of standing alone in the crowd.

Millicent spent the remainder of the brunch, taking the bishop by the arm, and introducing him to each one of the parishioners. They were all polite enough, but not interested in more than a 'hello, how are you, thanks for coming' conversation. It wasn't until she took him to old Mrs. Willoughsby that anything of substance was said. She told the bishop right out, leave the gay people alone. Millicent was astounded, the subject of homosexuality hadn't even been raised, but she blurted it out as if she desperately needed to make a point. This was often a characteristic of the elderly—and those who routinely conversed with them were quite used to it. The bishop simply smiled and took her hand in his.

After a short meeting with the vestry, the bishop said that it had been a long day and that he had best be home to Mrs. Walsingham. Derek and Millicent walked him out to his car.

"I can't say that I agree with your lifestyle Father, but the parish seems to be healthy enough."

"I can't say that I agree with your theology Bishop, but thank you for coming."

"Mother Millicent, please pray about your marriage. Perhaps something can be done. If there's anything that I can do, let me know."

Millicent, who had the fight drained out of her, just thanked the man, assuring him that she would indeed pray some more about it. The bishop waved as he got into his car, and Derek commented that he wasn't sure if he was blessing them, absolving them, telling them to go to hell, or what. He suggested that they go and pick up Colin, go to a movie. Preferably, a comedy that could take them away from the real world, at least temporarily.

They did just that, with the three of them laughing themselves silly that afternoon. When they got back to the rectory, they walked to a restaurant in Shadyside and they all had too much wine that night at dinner. It was in the evening that three staggering people were making there way back to the little Episcopal church in Friendship. Two of the people were still wearing the starched white linen collar that marked them as priests. Colin suggested that the bishop shouldn't come all that often, it was too hard on their livers. Then the two men stood with their arms around each other, as Millicent sadly made her way back to her house, and the husband whose love had grown cold.

Chapter 12

The parish soon got back to normal and Millicent finally decided to tell them of her decision to divorce her husband. Derek discreetly asked if Michael was to remain a member of the parish. Millicent's preliminary feelings about the matter was that he would probably leave the parish, he was a rather lukewarm Christian to begin with. After telling the vestry first, the day arrived when she decided to preach the sermon, and during that time, inform the parish of her decision.

The bishop was once again proved wrong, as the parish rallied around her, supporting her decision. Interestingly enough, Michael just slipped into the background. Colin wondered if he would ever just slip into the background if he and Derek were ever to break up. Derek recovered from the bishop's annual visitation and got back into the swing of things. He really hated it in Pittsburgh, a hatred that seemed to intensify after the confirmation ceremony. He began dropping little hints to Colin that they simply couldn't stay here much longer.

Colin was conflicted about the issue. He was willing to move away with Derek, the first man ever to elicit that kind of response from him, but he realized that, unless he had a comparable or higher paying job, it would be difficult. Derek also had to find work. Colin had learned a long time ago that his lover was not the best person in the world to sit around with nothing to do. It made him crazy, and this, in turn, made Colin crazy.

To add insult to injury, Colin's job had just become more stressful. Continued cuts forced layoffs. Past cost containment initiatives had left the staff with mostly people who had been employed there for a long time. Morale was at an all time low, and tempers were short. Medical people, especially among the supervisory staff, were somewhat petty to begin with, attention to detail among their attributes. When this was coupled low morale, the situation had become unbearable. For the first time since the early part of their relationship, he found himself being short and curt with Derek.

One Friday night he arrived home to find Millicent in the front living room.

"Hello Mother Millicent, how are you?" He asked mimicking the good bishop.

"Don't be trite Colin, it's very unbecoming a man of your age."

"And bitchiness is unbecoming a woman of your age. You have to be a lot younger to get away with it."

As the two were exchanging mutual insults, Derek happened to come into the room and hit the ceiling. "Why can't you two behave like adults, you especially Colin, after all that Millicent has been through. You could be a little more understanding."

"What do you mean, after all that she's been through. I'm a gay man, in case you have forgotten. It hasn't been easy, given my profession. Not to mention that fact that many of my friends have died of a horrible disease, which my current lover has. Couple this with the fact that you hate where we live, and bring it up to me every day, you might see why I can't understand the great trauma that she is having, especially since she will be receiving half of the community property. And why can't I just have had a bad day myself?"

The two priests stood in awe. Colin had never had an outburst like that with anyone present other than Derek. As he stomped up the stairs they looked at each other, dumbfounded. As Derek was about to apologize to Millicent for his lover's fit of anger, she beat him to the punch, saying: "What do you suppose has gotten into him?"

"I don't know. I'm sorry Millicent, he's never behaved that way, at least, outside of an argument with me."

"Maybe you're in the same boat that I was in – perhaps its time for you two to think about splitting up. Seems like he's a little abusive to me."

Derek knew that the only abusive part of their relationship was the abuse that he craved from his lover—in the dungeon. He also didn't like the way that Millicent was treating Colin, especially since the finality of her divorce loomed on the immediate horizon. While Colin was certainly not innocent in the tension between him and Millicent, he wasn't the sole problem either. So many times, Millicent had managed to project her feelings for her husband onto Derek, who then called Colin to task for some minor or merely perceived issue.

"Millicent, would you give him a break! You know, it can't

always be about us, and our feelings! There are other people in the world."

Millicent ran from the house in tears. Derek was upset with himself. Colin was upstairs playing *Les Miserables* very loudly. Derek hated *Les Mis*. Of course, he couldn't remember if he hated it for some personal reason, or if he hated it because Millicent hated it and taught him to hate it. He was surprised how many other people had an impact on his relationship. He could remember when he and Colin first got together, there were some tense times, primarily because Colin was still reeling from the bad relationship that he had with Tony. One night, when they were arguing, Colin had referred to Derek as Tony, a slip of the tongue. That slip taught Colin that he was letting Tony interfere with his and Derek's relationship. Derek had told him that some parts of the relationship only had room for the two people involved. Tonight, he learned the same thing for himself.

"CAN YOU TURN THAT DOWN, PLEASE?" Derek shouted to be heard over the lyrics of the musical.

Colin went over to the sound system and turned the volume way down. "Sorry, I didn't mean to blast you—just wanted to get away from myself."

"That's OK. I sort of owe you an apology."

That was all that he ever had to say to Colin. He never really had to apologize, he just had to acknowledge that Colin deserved one. As soon as he said that, Colin came over an embraced him. The two men kissed. It's odd how there may be long periods of time when two people in a relationship may have hot sex frequently, be intimate with one another, and truly a pair, but rarely kiss on the lips. Tonight, they both felt the intensity that a single kiss could hold.

"Let's go to a movie tonight," Colin suggested.

"No, let's save that for tomorrow. Let's go out tonight. We can call Al and see if he wants to go with us."

"Do you have designs on the cute Italian boy from down the street?"

"Well, that thought hadn't crossed my mind, but I know that he's your type."

"You're blond dear."

"Before you met me, how many of your lovers had dark hair and eyes?"

"All of them, but I often had sex with blond haired, blue eyed men as well."

"But you only professed love for dark haired men."

"So, you broke the mold, and now I could never go back."

"Before we can even think about going out though, I need a nap."

"Me too, it's been a rough week."

The two men ate, showered and climbed into bed at eight o'clock. Colin remembered to set the alarm for ten, the last time that they took a nap in preparation for a night on the town, they woke up at two in the morning with nothing to do, and fully rested. When the alarm rang, they groggily got up and Derek went to call Al. It was late, but he knew that Al hardly ever had anything to do on Saturday mornings.

Al was curled up on his bed, reading a novel when Derek called. At first he seemed a little hesitant to go to the bar with them, but he gave in and they agreed to pick him up at eleven. While no one was really talking about a three way, it was on the mind of all three of them. Derek was certainly willing, as was Al. The question remained, had Colin resolved his issues of having sex with a member of the Roman Catholic clergy? That question would have to be answered later, and probably would only be answered in action, and not words. Asking Colin at this point would certainly cause him to say no.

When they picked up Al, Colin and Derek were both stunned. They knew that he was a handsome man, they just didn't realize how hot he was in black leather. It was definitely due, in part, to the black hair and dark eyes, but, besides that, the man was simply stunning. Colin kept looking at him in the rear view mirror. They arrived at the bar after a few minutes and suffered through the usual sleazy banter that Brandy greeted them with each time that they came there.

Derek was still surprised that he couldn't forget Brandy's confession that fateful day of the memorial. He felt, in his heart, that he should have done something, but that was weeks ago. He also knew that, as a priest, he was bound by a sacred obligation to maintain the confidentiality of what he heard, but he also felt that justice should prevail. He was counting on God to do that—or to provide some way for Brandy to face the charges. As of the current date, God had remained silent on the matter.

The three men made quite an entrance. For once, Derek was dressed completely in leather. Colin had, up to this point, insisted that since Derek had taken the role of boy or slave in the community, that he could not wear leather jeans or chaps. While he wasn't really sure, he thought that somewhere along the way he had learned that there were old guard rules forbade boys from wearing leather pants. Three men in full leather, all of whom were quite attractive, caused a stir with their entrance. A leather club from another town was visiting—the tradition of the 'bar night'. Colin was happy that there were new faces in that bar, in addition to the same tired old people that he had been looking at every time that he entered this place for the past couple of years.

Dirk informed Colin that there was a play party that very night. Since it was a Friday, he knew that Derek had nothing to do the next morning, except spend the day with him. He wasn't sure how Al felt about orgies, but he would wait a little until he told them about it. He made sure that both men had enough to drink, but not too much. At midnight, as the bar started to clear out, he whispered to Derek about the play party that was to happen in an abandoned warehouse on the South Side. He then turned to Al and said, "Al, I'm not sure how to broach this subject, but there's a play party tonight. We can go if you want, or we can all go home, it's up to you. I don't want to force you to do anything that you don't want to do."

"I thought that you would never ask. I didn't know if you two did those things, and didn't want to suggest it and force you into something that would be uncomfortable for either of you. I heard about it in the bathroom when we first came in. I was struggling with the guilt of planning to sneak back out to it after you dropped me off at home. I couldn't think of any two people I would like to go to an orgy with than you two."

The grinning leather Master gathered his two boys and made his way to the car, leading the best looking two boys in the place out of the bar. Brandy was no where to be found, and Derek, for one, was glad that he didn't have to suffer through his insults and insipid greetings. Not to mention the fact that he didn't want to be reminded of his own private agony concerning the man. The trip to the South Side, while not far, involved coming down off a hill, and crossing one of Pittsburgh's three rivers. At one time, this part of town was where all of the steel mills were. They had long since been abandoned, and all but one had been torn down. The one remaining mill was in a neighboring community, out of sight from the center of the South Side business district. Most of the ground had been developed for something or another, sometimes a new business or yet another sports center for the city. The warehouse was a little to the west of the steel mill area, right in the center of the South Side. They entered from a doorway in a back alley. Colin was always amazed that the police didn't raid these things. Most of the neighborhoods in Pittsburgh were composed of older ethnic families who spent the better part of each day looking out their windows. The South Side had been predominately Polish or Slovak and there were still a lot of old men and women who monitored the goings on in their neighborhood. The sight of several carloads of men dressed in black leather entering an old warehouse in the middle of the night was sure to peak their curiosity. Yet, here was a true example of Pittsburgh's brand of tolerance—no one seemed to care, as long as it didn't intrude into their lives.

Once they entered the warehouse, a scene of complete decadence greeted them. There were scantily clad men in their twenties tied to St. Andrew's crosses being whipped and having hot wax dripped on them.. In a back corner, by a drain, naked men were kneeling while leather masters, still swathed in their leathers, pissed on them. There were slings where some of the men were being fucked while others were being fisted. It had been a while since either Colin or Derek had been confronted with such a display of outright sensuality.

They made their way to the 'meet and greet' area, a separate section where refreshments were served. A pornographic tape depicting much of what was going on in real life in the other rooms was playing. The men in this room were talking among themselves. In the other rooms, a code of silence prevailed, allowing only the commands of a Master to a slave to be spoken.

"Don't let me cramp your style, Al," Colin said as he handed the man a Diet Pepsi.

"Oh Sir, you could cramp anything of mine," was Al's reply.

As soon as Al called Colin 'Sir' the leather clad master felt a twinge in his crotch. He was definitely interested in Al sexually, and had decided to ignore is previous rule of not playing with a celibate priest. Derek noticed the change in his lover's behavior, smiling to himself. It had been a while since they had a sexual encounter with a third. To Derek, that was one of the things that kept the relationship healthy and on-going. They didn't have to be jealous of each other, or think about cheating, because they could experience it together.

Colin got them all more Diet Pepsis, and they spent a little time talking among themselves. After a while, he drifted back into the other areas, leading the two submissive men behind him. Most of the scenes were hotter from a distance than they were up close. There were also a few men who were at the play party who didn't have a clue, and would try a toy or flogger and end up giggling with their partner.

Colin led Al over to a secluded area where he strapped him to the wall. He handcuffed his lover and made him kneel. Derek watched as Colin took a flogger and began beating the man tied to the wall. At first, Colin was gentle, and the rhythm of the lashes matched Al's breathing, or perhaps it was the other way around. Soon the whips got harder and before long Colin was exerting himself as he flailed the other man's back. Al writhed in pain, and occasionally cried out. His pants were pulled down to his ankles, and his vest and T-shirt had been removed. His erection was plainly visible to both Colin and Derek. When he had enough, Colin untied Al, and restrained his hands behind his back. He led him to the still-kneeling Derek who received Al's dick in his mouth. As his lover sucked Al's dick, Colin kissed him on the mouth and held him tightly, the intimacy, a sharp contrast to the violent lashings of the flogger.

As they continued to play, others would stop by and try to join in. At one point, Al shook his head 'no' to indicate that they didn't want to be bothered. No one would approach Derek because of the locked leather collar around his neck. Colin didn't make eye contact with anyone except Derek and Al, which only added to the intensity of the scene. When it was Derek's turn at the cross, being on the receiving end of Colin's flogger, he found himself entering into the same rhythm that Al experienced as the leather thongs of the flogger hit his back. When the whipping intensified, he thought that he had entered ecstasy.

As Colin continued to flog Derek, Al asked permission to play with himself. Colin was hard——the flogging was exciting him almost as much as it was his lover. Before long something amazing happened, Derek came as Colin was flogging him. Almost simultaneously, Al came as well. Colin untied his lover, and, as Al took Colin's dick in his mouth, and Derek cradled his lover's balls in his mouth, Colin reached his orgasm very quickly after the other two men had reached their orgasms.

They didn't stay at the dungeon party long after that. They all three left, going back to Colin and Derek's house. They took showers, and Colin lent Al some sweats to wear. It was only two o'clock, but none of them was particularly tired. They climbed into the king size bed, and all started talking. There was an ease that the three men had as they lay there together, arms and legs entwined. Derek had seen this same ease with Vlad, but never this intense before, not even with Billy. It was as if Al was a kindred spirit. He knew that Colin liked Al, and that Al was attracted to Colin. He also knew that both men were comfortable with him. He didn't feel any jealousy at all with this man, and was surprised at the ease with which Colin accepted him. Colin was a very personable man, but always kept people at a distance until he invited them into his life.

Colin lay there thinking that the two men in his bed right now were each perfect in their own way. He couldn't believe that he had broken his proscription about having sex with a Roman Catholic priest. He wondered if the morning would bring the requisite guilt with it. Somehow, when something feels so good, guilt is often quickly forgotten. He was glad that they had done what they had done. He was also glad that Al was spending the night. It made it all seem so much more acceptable than dropping the man off at his house, and then speeding away into the night.

The next morning Al left, leaving Colin and Derek to spend some quality time together. The lovers spent their day in the usual manner, good shopping, naps, a meal cooked together, and tender sex followed by reading and an early night. As they were falling asleep, a very intoxicated Billy called.

"Hello Colin, what's up?" The young boy began, slurring his words.

"Not much, a quiet day here, Derek and I were just about to go to sleep."

"How come you guys never call me to play with you any more?"

"I thought that you were with someone now. You and that body builder from Columbus were getting pretty hot and heavy there for a while."

"Yeah, but that doesn't mean that I can't see you guys."

"Right, but seeing and playing are two different things, Billy. I thought that you said you wanted what Derek and I have."

"I do, but nobody wants to commit, at least not to me they don't."

"Well, if you tell them that you are part of an ongoing three way, they would even be slower to make up their mind."

"It works for you and Derek."

"Yeah, but it didn't start out this way, besides, leather relationships are a little different from regular ones. Most people don't have three ways that last more than part of the night."

"What he doesn't know, won't hurt him."

"It might, when he found out."

"I miss you guys."

"We miss you too, Billy, we really do. How about this, we can go to a movie or have dinner or even double date. But, as far as the playing, maybe we should avoid it until you decide if this thing is working with the guy from Columbus. You want a relationship, I'm really only looking out for you. Believe me, you are fun to play around with."

"You too, and so is Derek."

Colin was about to let Billy talk to Derek, but he looked over and saw that his lover was sleeping soundly. Colin couldn't help but wondering why Billy sounded so intoxicated. Maybe it was a combination of drugs and alcohol. When he first met Billy, the boy was always stoned, and used a little more recreational drugs than someone from Colin's generation was comfortable with.

They talked for a little while longer, and then said good night. Funny, if Colin wasn't with Derek, he might easily have been with Billy. Of course, the real romantic threat to their relationship had been Vlad. That man not only had the smoldering sensuality Colin liked, but he was truly a romantic. Colin was as well. Derek never used to be romantic at all, or in very small and measured doses. Now, since that period of time when he was so withdrawn, he seemed to be more and more interested in that side of the relationship.

As he was about to go to sleep, the phone rang. Thinking that it was the hospital, he immediately picked it up. It was Millicent, and she was crying.

"Is Derek there?"

Colin wondered why the woman could never acknowledge his existence on the phone. It made him angry. "He's asleep Millicent, should I wake him?"

"Yes. I need to talk to him," was her only reply.

He woke up his lover, handed him the phone and listened casually. When Derek handed him back the phone to hang it up, he told Colin that she was very distraught about the upcoming divorce. He would have to go and meet her for coffee. He then got up, dressed, kissed Colin good-bye, and was off. Colin was absolutely flabbergasted. He marveled at the hold Millicent seemed to have on Derek.

Chapter 13

Monday morning found Colin at his desk in his office at the hospital especially early. He and Derek didn't fight, per se, but Colin felt that Millicent had crossed a boundary. Derek spent the better part of Sunday and Sunday night consoling her. Colin said nothing, but went to bed early on Sunday evening and was in his office even before Martin arrived on the scene early Monday morning. As he was going through an intimidating stack of papers, Betty, one of the laboratory supervisors knocked on the door and poked her head in his office.

"I need to talk to you Mr. Morgan."

"Yes, Betty, what is it? And please call me Colin."

"You're probably going to get a letter from my staff today telling you all sorts of evil things about me."

Colin looked blankly at the woman across the desk from him. He didn't like her. He felt that she was incompetent, but had been there for so long that it wasn't funny. Firing her was out of the question, the court battle would be long and exhausting on many levels. He continued to stare at her, not knowing how to proceed. She didn't give him a chance to say anything, she continued on, all on her own.

"They're saying that I don't do my job, that I play favoritism, and that I'm dating my assistant. They say that I take long lunches and a whole bunch of other things."

"Betty, is any of it true?"

She was quiet for a moment. She simply stared at him. In many ways she reminded him of Baby Jane Hudson—she was getting older and her makeup was somewhat garish. Finally, she responded.

"I resent that, Mr. Morgan! I have worked hard for many years, and I don't deserve this whole thing, and I don't deserve being asked that by you."

"Betty, calm down. The simple fact is, I must ask that question. So I will ask it again, is any of it true? What are they basing their accusations on?"

"They're mad at me for firing someone, and for the fact that they didn't get very large raises, as if I had anything to do with that—that's more your area. They're just burnt out and taking it out on me."

"So you don't take long lunches, and you're not dating your assistant?"

"Absolutely not. And what business would it be of any of theirs who I am dating?"

For the first time in the conversation, Colin felt ill at ease. Betty was being just a little too defensive, and, ethical practice would dictate that a supervisor does not date a subordinate. He studied her closely noticing that she was clearly distraught. Hospital employees could be very mean and could carry out a vendetta against their supervisors. Usually, however, there was some strand of truth causing their actions. It was his job to discover those strands of truth in their complaint and to address it.

"Betty, I'll meet with your staff at ten this morning."

"Good, let's see them confront me with their accusations."

"No, I'll meet with them alone. Then, if you're needed, you can join us later."

"I don't think that's fair, Colin."

"Betty, that's the way that it's going to be and that's that. I want to ask them what is precipitating this action of theirs. They might be more open if you're not there."

She left angry and literally ran past Martin as he was coming into the office.

"A little tense for a Monday morning?"

"Oh Martin, just the usual."

"Well, it's probably going to be a little more tense for you, Tony's on the phone."

Colin couldn't believe his luck. It's early on a Monday, he had been at odds with his lover all weekend, the usual hospital pettiness was disturbing his well-being and now Tony—not much more could go wrong. He looked at the blinking light on his phone and tried to compose himself before picking up.

"Hello Tony, it's a little early for you. What's up?"

"Contrary to what you may believe Colin, other people besides you and your boy-toy priest work for a living."

Well, with those words a mean spirited   sentiment was obviously going to set the tone for this conversation. He just didn't believe that this was happening to him. Their relationship had deteriorated near the end, and they didn't leave each other on the best of terms. He didn't think that ex-lovers should interfere with each other once the thing was done. They lived in different cities and, from Colin's point of view, had little to say to each other.

"Well, what's up?"

"Who was that blond kid you were with in Columbus?"

"He is a friend."

"Are you two sleeping with him or whatever you call it in your disgusting sexual practices?"

"Not that it's any of your business, but no, we aren't," Colin replied, assuring himself that he was telling the truth since he used the present tense, and he and Derek were not currently having sex with Billy.

"I don't know if I believe you, but it's a good thing if you're not. He has been buying drugs in Columbus like there's no tomorrow."

Colin new that something was different about Billy the last time that he talked to him, late Saturday night. He wondered what it was that was causing Billy to revert to his old habits. He really had cleaned up his act, and Colin was happy that he had found the body builder of his dreams to settle down with. He knew that he would have to talk to him soon, but didn't want to come off like a parent, or, worse yet, like a person who was out of touch.

"Thank you for that information, Tony. Remember, he comes from a different generation that we do."

"Oh, so now you're saying that recreational drug use is OK?"

"I don't think that you and I have to debate the relative worth of recreational drug use. Is there anything else you wanted to bring up?"

"When will you be in Columbus again?"

"I'm not sure, why?"

"Well, you know, you could call. We could have dinner like civilized people, not just running into each other and me not knowing that you're in town."

"Tony, I'll consider it. But right now, I'm busy. Thanks for your concern."

He hung up the phone and buried his head in his hands. With this kind of start, it was promising to be one hell of a week. He hoped that his home life would be a little less confrontational than his professional and personal life had been so far this Monday morning.

The rest of the day passed quickly. He managed to have the meeting and, while the accusations of the staff weren't as bad as they had originally seemed, there was some truth to what they were saying about their supervisor. He would refer this problem to human resources to sort out and follow their recommendations.

As he pulled into the driveway, he noticed an old woman sitting on the porch of the rectory. He wasn't really in the mood to deal with a parishioner, but Colin always found it difficult to be short with older people or children. As he got closer, he realized that it was his grandmother. Intrepid, he assumed that she must have flown into Pittsburgh and taken a cab to the rectory, all at the age of eighty nine.

Mary Baird was a force to be reckoned with. Actually, the Lady Mary Baird was a force to be reckoned with, for she was truly a member of the Scottish aristocracy. Her whole life she had been known as Lady Mary Baird, and continued to use the title even after she came to the United States, which she still referred to as the colonies. It wasn't until the wife of President Johnson was known as Lady Bird Johnson that the Lady Mary Baird decided to drop the Lady. She felt that people would think that she was imitating the president's wife, and she certainly didn't want to be accused of that. The family called her 'mum', the kind of English slang for both 'mom' and 'ma'am'.

"Mum, what are you doing all by yourself on the front porch of an Episcopal rectory in Pittsburgh?" Colin said as he bounded up the steps to greet his grandmother.

"Well, I'm waiting for you. What do you think I'm doing? You forget that you may have been raised a Catholic, but I'm an Anglican through and through, and Anglican rectories have often been a part of my normal routine," she said in her crusty Scottish accent.

"What are you doing in Pittsburgh?"

"Visiting you on my way back to England. I thought that you boys would like to take an old woman out to dinner. It will probably be the last time that you see me alive."

"Well, Derek is at a meeting out of town right now, he won't be back until late."

"All the better, I hardly ever get to see you alone. I'm getting hungry and shouldn't go out alone. They don't let old people walk about on their own too much. So I can't rightly go out to dinner by myself.

People stare at old people when they are alone. Since it's only the two of us, I'll take you to dinner, but we better hurry, it's getting late."

"It's only five thirty, mum."

"Civilized people eat before the sun goes down."

"Well, then, come on, let's go."

Colin helped his grandmother into the car and then the two of them went to a restaurant high on Mount Washington, overlooking the city. The view was spectacular. There were many things that Derek could say about Pittsburgh, and many things that Colin could find wrong with it, but no one could deny that it was simply beautiful.

"How are you two doing, Colin? Are you happy?" The old woman asked peering into Colin's eyes as only the old could do.

"As happy as can be expected. Derek wants us to move, but we don't seem to have a good plan."

"Well, if it will make you happy, move. I spent my whole life in two places—the place where I grew up and the place that I was a married woman and then a widow. I can't help but thinking that I was missing something."

"I can't help but think that conventional wisdom would dictate that we have some sort of plan."

"Don't pay too close attention to conventional wisdom. Let me tell you something, Colin. You have to live your life the way that you see fit. Sometimes you make a mistake and sometimes you make a good move. You just go on and learn from it. I have always lived my life based on my sense of duty. Some people live based on their brains—that's what Derek does. You, smart as you are, live as your heart dictates. Wearing your heart on your sleeve like that can make you either very happy or very sad. You've got something good going here—listen to your heart. I've always admired you for that. Artists listen to their hearts, and I have never understood why you weren't some sort of artist."

Colin was amazed that this woman, born in Edwardian England, and committed to the principles of living with dignity, could be so insightful into the workings of the human heart. "That was good advice, Mum, of course, all of your advice is good."

"I know, I've lived a long time. People should listen to me more."

"Now, why do you think that this will be the last time that I see you alive?"

"I'm eighty nine for heaven's sake! Don't act feeble minded, I could go at anytime."

"Does Mom know that you're going to England?"

"No, and don't tell her."

"She will forbid me to go, or, worse yet still, decide to go with me. I'm old enough to go alone. If I die in England, so be it, you can all come over for the funeral and have a great party. I hear that the airlines give you a discount for a funeral."

"Like you need a discount."

"Not me—you. Which brings me to a subject I would like to bring up with you."

"Yes?" Colin asked, wondering where this was going.

"I'm going to give you a check for $150,000. That's half of your inheritance from me. The other half you get when I'm dead."

"Mum, you have to keep that money."

"Why? To buy a car that they won't let me drive? No way."

"But, there are tax consequences for both of us from that."

"Not at all, I've had my lawyer arrange this and he assures me that we are doing the right thing. I'm buying something from you."

"What would that be?"

"A small piece of property that you are selling me and that you will inherit. Please don't ask the specifics, there are more things involved than that –but the money is free and clear."

"Why? Why now?"

"So you can enjoy it—you and Derek could move and buy a nice place. That should take some of the edge off of your desire for a sound financial plan."

"But...."

"No buts, and don't you dare try to thank me. Take it, enjoy it. Do whatever you want with it, but please don't buy those Beany Baby things with it. I think those things are the craziest idea that anyone has ever thought of."

"I promise I won't do that," Colin answered, pondering his grandmother's non-sequitur.

The old woman paid for dinner and the two left for home. When they got back to the rectory, Derek was there. What a surprise it was for him to see Colin's grandmother. They chatted most of the evening, until about ten when she said that it was time for all old women to be in bed. She retired to the guest room and accepted Derek's offer to drive her to the airport the next morning.

As they got into bed, Derek grabbed his lover and kissed him. "I'm sorry about this weekend."

"That's OK Derek, you're torn between people who want some of your time. I know that."

"Sometimes you can be so understanding and sometimes you can be really unreasonable."

"Don't bring up bad things when I'm being understanding."

"OK, so how come your grandmother is here."

"She wanted to see us before she left for England, she thinks that her death is near."

"She'll probably outlive both of us."

"Yes, that's probably right. Oh, and she gave me $150,000."

"Yeah, right. And I've been appointed the Archbishop of Canterbury."

"Well, I don't know about that. That would make me Lady Canterbury, but we are a lot richer tonight than we were last night."

"Are you serious?" Derek asked incredulously.

"Very serious, Derek. The pressure is off, we can move any-time. Our living arrangements are at least partially taken care of."

It was too much for either of them to contemplate that night. They were both tired and were soon asleep. The next morning, Colin had breakfast with his lover and his grandmother, and after saying goodbye to her he left for work. Derek took her to the airport where they had a grand time, lamenting the passing of elegant air travel and playing a game that she always liked to play, 'where do you think they are going and why'.

That evening, the two men finally had the time to discuss Colin's windfall. After a dinner, which they shared, the first weekday dinner in a long time, as they were doing the dishes, Colin brought the subject up. "Well, we have some money now."

"Colin, we've always had money, we just have more, signifi-cantly more."

"I know, but it's enough to enable us to buy a house somewhere without having to worry about a mortgage, or, a very big mortgage at least."

"Right. I know."

"Aren't you happy about this, Derek?"

"Yes, I'm happy, but it's your money. You should do something that you want to do with it."

"I think that having a home with my lover would be something that I would like to do with it. A home in a place that would make both of us happy."

"We'd still have to work, Colin."

"I know. But we wouldn't have to worry about making a mortgage payment, or scraping money together to find a house."

"There are places that we could move where that would be just a down payment. The prices of houses in Chicago and San Francisco are much higher than they are here."

"Right, they are. But we wouldn't have to have a mansion. Just a house, or a condominium. A condo would probably be better any way, neither of us have much time to devote to maintaining the hearth and home."

"I know, but it's just so hard."

"Derek, what do you want to do? Do you wish to move?"

"Yes."

"Where?"

"I don't know. There's a process for me. It's not like you, just apply for a job and move. There has to be a church that needs a priest, and then the vestry actually has to choose you to be there."

"OK.......So, what do we do?"

"We could never live on my salary, Colin."

"Do you want to follow my career, then?"

"If I could find a job."

"Derek, we're not getting anywhere with this. It's like a big circular argument. I need to know what step to take next."

"Colin, just because you got some money, doesn't mean that we have to make a decision right now, does it? Let me check to see what's available, then we can see if there is anything for you in the same city. If there is, we apply. Then we move."

Colin was a little put off by the conversation. After his talk with his grandmother, and her admonition for him to follow his heart, he was ready to make changes in their lives so he and Derek could be happy. Derek, for once, was being the cautious one. Deep down, Colin knew that his lover was right. Right now though, he needed to dream and plan for the future. Why couldn't Derek ever humor him when he was like this?

They didn't talk any more about it that night. Derek knew that he was being a little obtuse with his lover. He just had so much on his mind. Millicent's emotional state was deteriorating every day, the bishop was on his case and, try as he might, he couldn't get the Brandy confession out of his mind. Colin was really being a nice guy these days, and a supportive lover, Derek just wished that he could be a little more emotionally available for him, but right now, he could not.

Colin couldn't figure out what the problem was this time. He was giving his lover everything that he wanted, but couldn't get him to join in making any future plans. That was the one and only problem in their relationship. Try as he might, Colin couldn't get Derek to open up to him on a regular basis. At first, he attributed it to Derek's HIV status. Colin always felt that he was somehow an outsider in a club that bonded positive men together. Then he thought that perhaps it was because of the disease that Derek found it difficult to enter into a deep, sharing and emotional relationship with another. Finally, Colin just thought that he was either too old for Derek or that there was some barrier that he put up in the early part of their relationship that had not yet been dismantled. Most of the time, it didn't matter to him. When a relationship is ninety percent good, you don't complain about the other ten percent. It was only on occasions like this that it bothered him.

That night, as Derek was attending another parish meeting, Al called. Colin was glad to hear from him. They had a long talk and agreed to meet whenever their schedules would permit, to have a frank conversation. Colin wanted to talk about Derek. Al wanted to talk about his feelings after their night together. Each of the men was looking forward to their meeting with a different agenda in mind. Al knew that Vlad had been a significant part of Colin and Derek's relationship and he wanted to see if the same situation could be possible for him. Colin just wanted someone to talk to—and, for the first time in their relationship, someone to complain to about Derek.

Chapter 14

A couple of weeks later, Colin and Al agreed to meet on a Wednesday night at the *Pirate's Nest*. Wednesdays were dead, as they are in most cities, and Colin thought that they would have ample opportunity for conversation. Derek was busy with, yet another meeting, this one in New York. He was on so many church committees, and it was beginning to be an intrusive element in their relationship. Colin was trying to simplify his life, for many reasons, while Derek was filling his up with professional activities. He would be out of town Wednesday through Friday. Colin didn't know this when he set up the meeting with Al.

Wednesday arrived and Colin saw his lover and Millicent off at the airport. He was conflicted about seeing Al that night—the man was so damned attractive! He told Derek about it, who thought that it was a great idea that they get together. He even alluded to the fact that they might end up in bed, and that he didn't mind that at all. This even made the conflict that Colin was feeling more intense. It's hard to meet someone with the intention of complaining about your lover, when your lover is being a saint about the whole thing.

Being a Wednesday, Colin thought that simplified leather was called for. He put on a black tee shirt, jeans, boots, and a black leather motorcycle jacket. He was surprised when he walked into the bar and Al was almost his mirror image, except that the tee shirt was white.

"Hello, Al, you are certainly an attractive man," Colin said as he accepted a drink from his friend.

"Hello, Sir."

"Al, could we dispense with the Old Guard formality, just for a bit?"

"Of course. I never know when to do what."

"Neither do I sometimes. Before I met Derek, I was fairly rigid in my own following of protocol. There's something different about loving a man and only interacting on the basest level of sexual dominance and submission. Now, half of the time, I don't know if I'm being a top, a husband, a lover, a partner, or just totally not myself."

"Colin, I have always wondered what it would be like to be in a leather relationship. I mean all of the boy-sir stuff has to get old after a time."

"Well, I don't know if Derek and I are doing it right or not. I really think that the level of protocol and adherence to role has to be worked out by the two people in the relationship."

"From what I understand, you guys often have more than just the two of you in the relationship."

"That's right. That's part of the beauty of leather relationships. They tend to challenge our concept of a loving marriage. There are leather families where there are several boys and one top, or several tops and several boys."

"Seems like heaven to me."

"My good Father, I am surprised at you!" Colin said in mock surprise. "And you with your commitment to celibacy and all."

"Well, that commitment was made when I was quite young. Sometimes I think I should revisit that decision."

"But you're the perfect priest, at least in my eyes."

"You don't know the current thought on perfection in the priesthood in the Roman Catholic Church."

"You forget. I studied for the Roman Catholic priesthood."

"You're kidding me! I thought that you were born and raised an Episcopalian."

"No, I was a Catholic. I became an Episcopalian because I married an Episcopalian priest. But I am sorry to hear about your current doubts."

"They're not really doubts. It's just that I want what you and Derek have. It seems like such an authentic relationship."

Recognizing his cue, Colin decided to broach the subject. "Al, it's not perfect. We struggle every day, sometimes less than others. It's hard. Sometimes I wonder about the ability of two men—each with their own ego that needs nourishing, to have a relationship. At least the kind of relationship that we have been exposed to with our heterosexual friends."

"But you and Derek seem totally happy."

"No relationship is perfect. And remember, we bring all of those ideas that we learn from our parents into the thing, and it just doesn't work. Gay liberation has been wonderful, but it hasn't been until now that we are truly beginning to form our culture, and paving the way in relationships isn't easy."

"Colin, come on. Is it that bad?"

"No, sometimes I just wish we could communicate a little better. He gets entrenched behind the walls that he builds, then I get defensive, then we fight."

"I hear it from my straight parishioners and my gay friends. The problem isn't gay or straight, it's our society. Sometimes I think that we've forgotten how to communicate. Or, some of us communicate too much, analyze too much, process too much."

It was there, in that tacky leather bar in Pittsburgh on a Wednesday night, that Colin realized that he was being a baby about the whole thing. There, with this renegade priest who had eyes that could melt a glacier, he realized how lucky he was to have Derek. And how enviable their life together really was. Why did he think that just because he was a gay man that the coming together of two people should be ideal. Of course there were rough edges that had to be smoothed down. It was as if a weight had been lifted from his shoulders, and coupled with the few drinks that the two men had shared, Colin felt like himself again—horny.

"So Al, what are you going to do about your situation?"

"Derek thinks that I should become an Episcopal priest."

"I thought that proselytizing was frowned on in the current ecumenical environment."

"Just a suggestion that he gave."

"He never even mentioned it to me, his lover."

"Of course not, we priests do keep confidences, you know. . . He probably also didn't mention that I was completely bowled over by our last encounter. It was so hot. Then the cuddling, I couldn't believe it."

"I was impressed myself."

"We should do it again."

"Well Al, there this leather top who's without his boy tonight and could use a little servicing."

"And I have the boy's permission to service you, Sir."

"Since when do boys give permission?"

"It's a boy-boy thing. Of course we wouldn't do anything without first consulting you," Al replied, grinning the whole time.

"Then what are we doing wasting our time here?"

"I thought that you would never ask, Sir."

The two men left the bar and, in separate cars, returned to Colin and Derek's house. Since the driveway of the house was hidden from the public, Colin decided to put Al through his paces. When the hot Italian got out of his car, Colin's gloved hands pushed him to his knees.

"I think that it's time for you to lick some boot, boy."

Al was down on his hands and knees, his tongue massaging the top of Colin's boots. Colin was always amazed at how sensuous that felt. It not only looked good, but he could actually feel it in his toes. He pulled out his cock, and before Al even raised his head, a steady stream of piss covered him. When he was done he put his cock away and told Al to crawl into the house.

By the time that the two men made it to the basement dungeon, their hard-ons were plainly visible.

"Take off your clothes, boy."

Al did as he was told, and folded the wet tee shirt and jeans in the corner. Colin gently put a leather collar on him, then a hood that contained a gag and a blindfold. Once it was secured, he grabbed leather hand restraints and tied Al's hands behind his back. Then, even more gently than before, he pushed the naked man's head down to the floor and pulled a flogger off the wall. He began to whip Al, gently at first, and then with increasing intensity.

Colin couldn't really tell if the moans coming from under the hood were moans of joy or of pain, but the erection sticking out from the naked man made him think that they were the result of joy. Or, if not joy, at least ecstasy. He pulled out his own cock, and removing the gag from the hood, shoved his cock as far as he could down the man's throat. He could have cum at that very moment, the intensity of the scene was overpowering, but he decided to wait.

The Master then pulled the naked man up and guided him to a leather covered saw horse. He secured his feet to one side and his hands to the other so that the man's ass was up in the air as he was bent over the horse. After he put on a condom and lube, he undid the hood so he could see Al's face when the slave would turn his head. Colin didn't wait for the preliminaries, this wasn't about making love, this was fucking. He pushed his cock right in and the other man let out a yell. That only made Colin want to do it more, and harder. Try as he might to prolong the scene, Colin came rather quickly. He reached under Al to finish him off, but the man had already cum. As a matter of fact, Al came right when Colin stuck his cock in his ass.

Colin reached over and undid the restraints. Al was weak in the knees from the scene. He turned around and literally fell into Colin's arms. The two remained there, embracing for a long time. Then Colin said, "If you go up stairs and take a shower boy, you can sleep with me tonight."

"Yes Sir," Al replied as he turned and went to the shower.

Colin picked up Al's clothes and threw them into the washer. He wiped off his jacket and boots. He surprised himself. Usually this was the boy's responsibility. In the past, he had only done this for Derek, out of pity for Derek when he was tired. By the time that he made it to the bedroom, Al was kneeling, naked beside the bed.

"Get in boy."

They then got into the big bed and found each other's arms. Just as they began to kiss, the phone range. Colin reached to pick it up, "Hello?"

"Hello Sir, are you doing OK?" Derek said on the other end.

"Why, yes........." Colin clearly didn't know what to say next. He knew that Derek had given him permission to play with Al, but he didn't want to rub it in his face.

"Would you like me to talk you through a little orgasm, baby?" Derek teased, knowing that Al must be somewhere in the house, possibly tied up.

"Derek............."

"I know. Al and I had this arranged."

"But how did you know that I would do it? And how did you know that we were done?"

"Done? You've got to be kidding. I thought that you would just be starting and going all night. Is my lover becoming an old man, tiring out early in the evening?"

"No, but that hot Italian butt does the trick."

"Colin, I'm glad that you two played around. You get so bitchy when I'm away, and besides, I like Al. And this is the first one that I got to pick."

"One? What have you picked?"

"You know what I mean, usually it's you that decides who we

play with, I like him."

"Well, as long as you don't like him too much."

"You're the one in bed with him, my love."

Colin burst into laughter and he and Derek continued on for a few minutes before saying that they loved each other and then good-night. After he hung up, Colin reached over and kissed Al passionately on the mouth. "That's from Derek."

The next morning, Al had to leave early. Colin did something that he hardly ever did, he called in sick. He just couldn't bear the thought of dealing with Betty and her problems, or anyone else for that matter. He needed a day to himself. He went out to breakfast, then to the mall, took in a movie, stopped by the local gay bookstore, and bought a novel. Before returning home, he picked up some Chinese food. Finally, when he had all of his supplies, he went home. That night he took a bubble bath—laughing the whole time. A big leather top sitting in a tub full of freesia bubbles caused him more than a little cognitive dissonance. Then he put on boxers and a tee shirt, turned the air conditioning way up, crawled into bed to read. Before he went to sleep, he decided that he wouldn't go to work the next day either. Why go in just for Friday? He deserved a break, and since this was something that he rarely did, he didn't feel any guilt. Amazingly enough, he didn't feel too much guilt about sleeping with Al either. Not only the guilt about being with someone other than Derek, even with Derek's permission, but also the guilt associated with Al's profession. It saddened Colin that Al would consider leaving the church, but, at the same time, he realized that the man had to have some peace in his life. If what you do, or what you want to do, is opposed to what you are, it can become disconcerting. He knew that it was hard to leave Catholicism. Colin wondered what it would take to convince the church that homosexuality was just another expression of human sexuality, neutral in and of itself, but different. He doubted that he would ever see that change. It was then that he recalled his last conversation with Bishop Walsingham. Why was it, at this point in history that the test of authenticity in Christianity revolved around your position on homosexuality? He would never know. However, he did know that his lover returned tomorrow, and, with the day off, he could really prepare a coming home feast for him.

Chapter 15

The weeks after Colin's midweek encounter with Al were glorious, as far as he and Derek were concerned. Al joined them regularly for drinks, dinner, and sex. Sometimes he just came over to hang out. When one of the three was busy, the other two were usually together, doing something. And sometimes, that something was just sitting quietly, reading. Billy, feeling neglected at first, rekindled his relationship with the body builder from Columbus. Colin thought that if his and Derek's life together were some medieval chronicle, it would read, and there was peace in the land.

Millicent had finally divorced Michael Barclay, with the parish's support. He, mercifully, decided to attend church at another parish. Remarkably, after the divorce, she became less intrusive in Derek's life. She felt that it was time to move on, and was beginning the process of looking for work elsewhere. Colin found the whole procedure rather cumbersome, but it was the way that the Episcopal church worked. He knew that when it was time for them to move on, Derek would have to submit to the same process, which could be dragged out for months, in some cases.

Al began studying the theology and politic of the Episcopal church, having begun a leave of absence from his own ministry. Colin was particularly understanding of Al at this time. Leaving the Catholic Church, especially for a priest, is not an easy thing. And not something that should be undertaken without a great deal of soul searching. That was what Al was doing these days, searching his soul for an answer. But he was doing it in good company.

Derek, with Al in the picture, finally began breaking down the walls that he had constructed around himself, and he and Colin were closer than ever. He was still fighting his own demons regarding Vlad's death and Brandy's confession, but they didn't seem as painful as the time passed. They still went to the bar occasionally, but they certainly weren't fixtures there. Every time that they went, Colin always remarked that the same people, wearing the same clothes, were sitting in the same spots at the bar.

Brandy was trying his best to have a leather contest held in Pittsburgh, at his bar. It was an uphill battle. He could fool the leather community in Pittsburgh that he was a major figure in the S/M world, but the rest of the country knew better. When he made requests, he was usually turned down, with people just commenting that they never heard of this guy.

The pressure was off about the two deaths that occurred at his hands. Time had made the local crowd forget about them. This became especially true after another group in town caused some serious medical damage to a man at one of their local gatherings. This, while not intentional, certainly was the result of someone trying something that they didn't know how to do. In this case, it was a top telling a bottom that he really did know how to fist someone in a sling, when he had no clue what he was doing. At that time, the rest of the community remembered the Vlad incident. They concluded that an incompetent top could do a lot of harm. Meetings were held and lectures on leather techniques were scheduled. Colin was asked to help with the instructional part, conducting demonstrations of various techniques. He just laughed as he declined, saying that his demonstrations were usually done one on one.

It was a Tuesday in early August when the Episcopal Bishop paid an unannounced call at St. Swithen's Rectory. Being August, there wasn't much going on in the parish that night, and Colin and Derek were preparing dinner with Al. When the doorbell rang, Al went to answer it.

"Hello, I don't think that I know you," said the bishop.

"Oh, I'm sorry, I'm Al D'Amore," he replied.

"I'm Bishop Walsingham, Al, it's nice to meet you. I'm looking for the Rector."

"Oh, he and Colin are in the kitchen, come with me."

At this point, the Bishop was rather in the dark about who Al D'Amore was. He was hoping beyond all hopes that he was either a parishioner, or that he was someone about to break up Colin and Derek so the horrible homosexual priest would finally leave his jurisdiction. Dutifully he followed Al into the kitchen.

"Good Evening," the bishop announced as he entered the picturesque kitchen.

"Hello, Bishop, this is a surprise!" Derek stood up, hating himself for doing that.

"Hello Bishop, nice to see you again," chimed in Colin, knowing that he would pay for that 'nice to see you again' when he and Derek were alone later.

"Well, it looks like a bachelor night in the kitchen," said the bishop, realizing that he just put his foot in his mouth.

"We were just preparing dinner, would you care to join us?" Colin said, already feeling the daggers that his lover was throwing with his eyes.

"No, I'm sorry, I can't really stay. Mrs. Walsingham is expecting me at home. I just came to talk about parish finances for a few minutes with the Rector.

"Oh, let me excuse myself then, come on Al, let's go get something for desert tonight," Colin quickly interjected.

"Thank you Colin. Father?" The Bishop said, looking at Derek.

Before he could even think, as Derek said yes, so did Al. He was just so used to answering to Father that he did so out of habit. He and Derek answering at the same time,

"Yes?"

There was a moment of silence, as deafening as a tornado. The Bishop quickly added, "Oh, you're a priest as well?"

"Yes Bishop, I am."

"Local?" Asked the bishop.

"Yes local bishop, but I am a Roman Catholic priest."

"How nice of you to visit the local Episcopal parish, I love it when there is interaction between our two churches."

Colin had to hide his smile, thinking of the interaction that he, Derek and Al had been having over the past few months. Derek, for his part, was remaining silent, hoping that Al would do so as well.

"However bishop, I am thinking about leaving the Roman church and joining yours," Al added, trying to fill in the dead space between them with something-----anything. Derek felt doomed.

The bishop looked a little perplexed. It wasn't that he was opposed to people changing religions, he was just in an awkward situation. It wouldn't do much for Catholic/Episcopal relations in the area to have a renegade priest in his flock. "That's a very drastic step, Father. May I ask what it is that is causing you to think about this?"

At this point, both Colin and Derek were hoping that Al would remain silent, or at least, evasive. They had, many times, told Al about Derek's problems with the local bishop. However, they realized that the good Italian boy was feeling the first stirrings of liberation, and he was proud to discuss, with anyone, friend or foe, his new found feelings of pride in his sexuality.

"I'm gay, bishop, and I think that I might be happier in a church with a less rigid stand on the issue. And I also don't think that I can remain celibate."

If the previous silence was deafening, this one was deadening. Derek could see the storm clouds brewing in the Bishop's eyes. Colin knew that this was just not a good situation, and Al was confronting his oppressor for the first time, having dreamed of the freedom that coming out publicly would win for him. What had once been concealed must now, in Al's opinion, be revealed. No one spoke. Colin looked at his feet. Al looked at the Bishop. Derek looked at his hands, and the Bishop looked at a spot about two feet above Al's head. Someone had to do something.

"Bishop, I believe that you wanted to talk to me about parish finances?" Derek asked, finally getting the nerve to change the subject. The bishop didn't respond.

"Bishop? May we retire to my office, and I can get you any information that you would like," he added. The Bishop still didn't respond.

"Bishop, would you like a drink of water, or something stronger?" Colin asked, truly interested in the man's well being. The bishop still said nothing. So the four men stood around in the rectory kitchen, each uncomfortable in their own way. Finally, the elder cleric spoke:

"Father Al, I think that you might be misinformed about the current state of moral theology and teaching in the Episcopal church, and I can understand why, given the references that you have come into contact with. However, I must tell you that homosexuality is not condoned by the church, and homosexual clergy are only tolerated in some dioceses, this not being one of them. You should consider your own vocation without the influence of outside distractions." The Bishop now looked Al directly in the eyes.

"I disagree with you Bishop. I think that you are adopting a very un-Christian stance in this whole issue. It is because of *your* attitude that gay people are still being attacked and killed by Christians who feel that it is their right to do away with the abomination before the Lord. I don't see anything in the Gospels about homosexuality, only about approaching each other with love. How dare you stand before me and condemn me because of the person I love." When Al was finished, he stared directly back into the Bishop's eyes.

The group returned to silence. It was clearly the bishop's turn to respond. After a few minutes, he turned to Derek and said, "Father, this is not a good time to discuss our business. I'll have my office set up an appointment to have you and the vestry come to the diocesan offices to discuss this. I think that it's time that I return to my home, and my wife."

He stood there, not on ceremony, but making the point that he had the right to be shown out and not to leave on his own. Derek, boiling with anger at the bishop's words did not want to show the man any respect and stood his ground. Al was too angry to do anything but stand there and glare at the bishop. Colin finally broke the spell and said, "Bishop, let me show you to the door."

The two men left the kitchen, leaving the two priests alone. Colin quietly led the bishop to the rectory door, and then opened it for him. He shook the bishop's hand and said good-bye, neither man knowing quite the words to use to conclude the evening's conversations.

When he returned to the kitchen, he found his lover and his friend standing, each still reeling from the anger of the encounter that they had just experienced together. "Well, that went rather well, don't you think?" He said trying to break the tension.

At first Derek looked at him as if he had just said the most horrible thing in the world. Then Al started to giggle, and before he could stop himself, so did Derek. After a couple of minutes, all three men were doubled over in laughter. That night they prepared a wonderful dinner and went to a coffee shop in Bloomfield for desert, since Colin and Al never did get to leave to go get something from the bakery.

Recounting the events of the evening, Derek and Al began to get angry all over again. Colin, while he understood their anger, did not understand its intensity. Colin, unlike his lover, had no problem when he discovered that he was gay. He simply made the appropriate changes in his life and went about having sex with men. Derek and Al agonized over the decision, denying it at first, and then, after a troubled journey, finally accepting it. Derek always secretly admired his lover's ability to make the transition so easily.

That night the three men discussed, and sometimes argued about the degree of acceptance of others' ideas in the gay community. Derek and Al made a strong point that homosexuality should not be the watermark of orthodoxy in Christianity. Colin, taking the devil's advocate position, argued that while he agreed with that, there was still the possibility for disagreement, and that acceptance of homosexuality shouldn't necessarily be an indication of enlightenment. He didn't really believe that, but he believed that he should try to defend, not the bishop's opinion, but the belief system that led the man to that conclusion.

By the end of the evening, all three men had found a new, and deeper intimacy. The kind of intimacy that comes when people open themselves up and reveal their innermost beliefs to one another. Derek knew that he had fired the final shot that would cause a personal confrontation with the bishop. Colin knew that as well, but didn't say anything. Al realized that he had just taken a step that was somewhat irreversible, he was sure that this bishop would call his bishop and recount the whole thing. He felt relieved and scared, and was glad when Colin suggested that they all go home and spend the rest of the night together. They did just that.

That night there was no major sex scene in the dungeon, or in the bed for that matter. Oh, there was sex. No one could be in the same room with Colin without some sort of sex on some level. But it was sex that involved holding, and kissing, and caressing. There was no real goal of this kind of sex—no path leading to ecstasy, just a joy of sharing the touch of another person. That night the three of them fell asleep, Al in the middle, getting the support of the two men that he had come to love. Colin and Derek knew that they too were taking a step, inviting another into their life more deeply than anyone else had ever been invited. It was comforting and frightening at the same time. Not one of the men had a clue where it would eventually lead. But they were willing to take the first steps in a new path on their journey together. It was Colin who knew that whatever happened, it would probably entail moving to another city, Derek, whether he knew it or not, had just burnt his professional bridge in Pittsburgh.

Chapter 16

A couple of Fridays later, Colin decided that it was time for a night on the town. Since Al was more or less living in their house right now, he called him from work, told him to track down Derek and declare Friday night through Sunday morning 'family time'. It had been a while since they had been to a bar, any bar, and he thought that they might begin at the *Pirate's Nest* that night. Al was surprised, since Colin rarely liked to put on leather in the dead of summer, and he wouldn't bend the rules enough to do away with it for a night, not on a weekend.

That night, Colin arrived home on time to find Al and Derek, naked, with collars on, in the kitchen, having just prepared a meal. The sight of the two men in total submission let Colin know that the tone was set for the weekend—this was going to be about serious leather. He ate his meal that night in silence, attended by two very attractive slave boys. The mood was now definitely set. The boys had prepared the scenario, and he was going along with it. He wouldn't do anything to destroy it. After dinner, while the two slave boys cleaned the kitchen, Colin took a nap. As soon as the sun went down, he was up, showering and spending a little more time than usual getting ready to go out.

He picked a black tee shirt, leather chaps and vest, with motorcycle boots and leather police gloves completing the picture. He wouldn't wear a leather cap tonight – he still could manage a boyish look in the dim lighting of the bar, and thought that it would be sexy, especially since he was the eldest person of the trio. The two boys knew what they were to wear: white tee shirts, with jeans, boots and a leather vest. Most Old Guard leather Masters liked to see their submissive men dressed like that in the bar.

When they were all dressed, Derek and Al knelt at Colin's feet with their leather collars in their hands. Colin fastened Derek's first, then Al's. To Derek's he attached a small padlock in the back and locked it. Tonight was going to be all about ritual and protocol. All three men knew the significance of the two types of collars. The collars meant that they were Colin's property, that they couldn't speak to others without permission and that no one had the right to speak to them, let alone touch them. The unlocked collar on Al meant that he could 'play' with another if permission were granted, and it wasn't likely that permission would be granted tonight. The locked collar on Derek meant that he was to be left alone—he could only 'play' with someone else upon the direct order of his Master—Colin.

Derek and Al had already set up the toys in the basement dungeon. They actually had a great time all day setting the scene for tonight's activities. Derek knew that Colin needed a little ego boost, and thought that this was one way he was sure to get that from him. He also knew that the three of them needed a little old fashioned S/M in their lives. When people spend each day together, it is sometimes difficult to recapture the mood. They had set the stage and Colin was happily participating in it. Derek knew that it was as much for him as it was for Colin. He needed to be reminded from time to time of their roles, and would often dream of living a life in total submission to another man. He knew that it would probably be more drudgery than he was fantasizing about, but he still had that nagging desire to have that kind of relationship. He also knew that Colin was wise to mitigate those rigid rules. Derek knew that even the most devoted slave needed a break from them, and, he wasn't sure that he himself could maintain that strict adherence to role for an extended period of time.

As he got the keys to his car, Al handed him a remote control. Looking perplexed, he stared at the two men.

"Permission to speak, Sir," Derek said.

"Yes, Boy, what is it?"

"A present Sir, this is the control for a remote TENS unit. The other boy and I have place the electrodes where we thought that you would like them."

Colin smiled a little, without giving in to a level of intimacy that would destroy the current mood. He always wanted a remote TENS unit. He thought that it would be fun to apply the current from across the room and send the little shock through a slave's testicles without warning. If anything, he was a playful leather top, always looking for ways to interject a little fun into the play. Derek and Al must have purchased this through one of the mail order leather supply houses. This was definitely going to be a fun night.

"Thank you boys. Let's get going."

Derek locked the door behind them and waited as Colin got the car. The two 'boys' sat in the back, in silence. Colin drove the car in silence. They parked in the parking lot surrounded by the large chain link fence on the very top of the Hill District in Pittsburgh. It was a beautiful night and the downtown area could be seen, the lights of the buildings veiled in the gauze of a hazy summer night.

Derek and Al followed behind Colin as he led the way into the bar. They expected to be stopped by Brandy at the entrance, but, surprisingly enough, he wasn't there. They walked into the dimly lit space and Colin handed Derek a bill and sent him up to the bar to get three beers. He really wanted to activate the TENS unit when Derek was balancing the three bottles on his way back, but he thought that perhaps he should wait.

Once they all had their beers, Colin instructed Derek and Al to kneel, one on each side. Dirk was the first in the bar to realize that there was some serious leather play going on in Colin's favorite corner and came over.

"Hello Sir, if you need assistance with these two, let me know. I can certainly be of help," he said, grinning from ear to ear.

"I'll keep that in mind Dirk, but I'm pretty sure that I can handle it tonight."

Just as he finished speaking, Colin pressed the TENS button, which was set on half power. The two kneeling men jumped and groaned. Colin just smiled. Dirk looked a little confused until Colin showed him the control.

"What brought about this serious level of intensity, Colin?" Dirk asked.

"I'm not sure. Actually, most of this was their idea. I kind of like it, I haven't seen this much submission since my last trip to a leather bar in Amsterdam."

"Can I play with the control?"

At first, Colin wanted to decline, but when he saw the look of disgust on Derek's face he handed Dirk the control. Derek thought that Dirk was an idiot, and didn't want to have any kind of sexual interaction with him. Colin mostly agreed with Derek's assessment, but was a little more patient with Dirk than his lover was, especially about Dirk's relative lack of intelligence. Tonight, he thought that he would show Derek a little of what it would be like to be at the total mercy of another man. As he watched, Dirk went about using the TENS unit with abandon. As a matter of fact, Dirk played a little too much with the controls from Colin's point of view, somewhat like a bored man playing with the remote control for the television set. After about ten minutes of watching the two men that he cared for jumping around over and over again, Colin retrieved the control and let Derek and Al rest for a minute.

"Remember Dirk, too much is as bad as too little when it comes to a TENS unit," Colin said as he put it in his back pocket.

Various members of the local leather club came by, mostly to stare at Derek and Al kneeling on the floor. Some exchanged pleasantries with Colin, some retreated into the shadows, groping each other's crotches, having been turned on by the public display that Colin, Derek and Al were putting on.

When Dirk came back to the group, Colin asked, "Have you seen Billy around lately, or is he spending all of his time in Columbus these days?"

"Actually I didn't see him very much at all until tonight. He was here a little earlier, and drunk as a skunk," Dirk answered.

"That's a shame, he must be having problems with that body builder of his, but he insists on having a body builder. I don't understand the younger generation, they are so specific in their requirements for the perfect man," Colin replied.

"Well, he certainly didn't get the perfect man tonight. He went home with Brandy. It looked like Christmas morning for Brandy."

Before Colin could even begin to express his dismay at what he had just heard, Derek was on his feet, looking right at Dirk and saying, "Who did Billy go home with?"

Colin went to put his hand on Derek's shoulder to push him down to his knees. "Hold on boy, who gave you permission to speak?"

"This is serious Colin. Dirk, who did you say that Billy went home with?"

"Brandy, boy. But you better watch your position or your Master is really going to let you have it tonight," Dirk said, smiling.

Derek had a look of total fear in his eyes. Colin had never seen him react this way. He grabbed Dirk's arm and repeated, "Who did Billy go home with?"

"Brandy, Derek, calm down, he's not the greatest, but its not like he went home with Jack the Ripper," Dirk said, looking at Colin with upraised eyebrows.

"Colin, you have to go to Billy's house now and stop them!" Derek cried.

"Derek, what's wrong? I've never seen you like this," Colin said, grabbing his lover's hand.

By now, Al was standing and trying to comfort Derek. Nobody knew what was wrong with him. Derek couldn't believe the position that he was in. He couldn't tell Colin why he had to go to Billy's house, he just knew that someone had to go over there and interrupt them before Brandy could kill Billy. For one brief moment, he thought of breaking the silence required by his church. He started to cry. Colin was moved by this uncharacteristic display of emotion from his lover.

"OK Derek, I'll go. Please calm down. I'll go and tell Brandy to leave Billy alone. But I will feel like a fool."

"Hurry Colin, please hurry."

"Are you guys coming with me?"

"No, just go—we'll meet you back home."

Colin ran out of the bar and got into his car quickly. He was so confused, he had never seen Derek this upset. Usually he would reason with his lover if he thought that he was being unreasonable about something, but Derek was so upset that he just decided to do as he asked. He hoped that Al could calm him down by the time that he got back home – probably with Billy in tow. He sped through the town on his way to Billy's apartment in Squirrel Hill. Derek probably didn't know that Colin had a key to Billy's apartment, and he was pondering whether he was going to use the key or not. He just guessed that he would cross that bridge when he got to it.

It wasn't long before he was standing outside Billy's apartment, ringing the bell. There was no answer. That wasn't surprising. What person in their right mind would leave a hot sex scene, late on a Friday night, to answer an unexpected guest. He tried calling Billy on his cell phone, but there was no answer. Colin didn't feel comfortable using the key to get into Billy's apartment, there was a boundary that he just didn't think he should cross. It wasn't that he thought that Billy should be with Brandy, Brandy was pure slime, and Billy could do much better. But Colin's dilemma was, do you overstep your bounds simply because you think that someone's trick is tacky?

He made his final decision when he closed his eyes and remembered the terror that he saw in Derek's face. He wasn't sure what was going on, but he knew that Derek didn't get that upset so easily. As he reached for the key he was thinking of all the reasons Derek could have for not wanting Billy to have sex with Brandy. The only one that he could come up with was that Brandy was HIV positive and didn't practice safe sex, and that Derek somehow knew this.

He opened the door to Billy's apartment hearing the music that Billy always played to drown out the sounds of sex so his neighbors couldn't hear the moans, groans, commands, and groveling. The apartment was totally lit with candlelight and Colin knew that Billy and Brandy were in the back bedroom, the one that Billy had decorated for sex. He didn't know if he should clear his throat, call out, or what. Perhaps he should just walk in acting like he was Billy's master and that some protocol had been broken. Of course, Billy could end up never talking to him again, but that was the chance that Colin was going to take—taking that chance only because of his lover's apparent distress.

He entered the hallway and heard Billy groaning in the next room. He also heard Brandy's voice.

"Die you son-of-a-bitch cock sucker! Die!" Brandy's voice came through the door.

Still, Colin wasn't particularly alarmed. An S/M scene was sometimes a fantasy built on terror. Usually the two parties were merely acting, but Billy didn't seem to be able to respond. Perhaps Brandy was some 'fright freak' and had Billy gagged as he was pretending the threaten him.

When Colin opened the door, he was shocked, and was momentarily unable to respond. Billy was naked, his face was bleeding. He feet were tied together and his hands were handcuffed behind his back with the cuffs being tied to the rope that had bound his feet. He mouth was covered with a thick piece of duct tape. There was a rope with a noose around his neck and Brandy was standing over him, pulling up tighter and tighter on the rope. Billy's face was turning blue, and his eyes were not only terrified, but appeared to be bulging from their sockets.

"What the fuck are you doing here asshole?" Brandy spit at Colin.

"Let him go, you stupid fuck," was Colin's reply as he jumped across the room and punched Brandy squarely in the face.

Now Colin rarely fought, as a matter of fact, he couldn't remember any time in his life when he had hit anyone. He was, however, very strong, and his punch had a significant impact on Brandy, who fell backwards, dropping the rope that was attached to Billy's neck. Colin went to reach over and remove the noose, when Brandy picked up a box and threw it at Colin, missing him.

Once the rope was removed, Billy doubled over on the floor, choking through the duct tape. Colin knew that he had to remove that tape soon, or Billy might choke on his own spit, but Brandy was still fighting him off. As the two men rolled around on the floor, they didn't hear the sirens coming up the street. Within minutes, three City of Pittsburgh police were in the room with guns drawn. Derek and Al appeared a short time later, and were peering through the door.

Brandy knew that he had been caught, and quietly raised his hands. The police still didn't know what was going on, or who was the real villain. Quickly Derek entered the room, shouting, "Don't shoot. It's him," pointing to Brandy.

By now, Colin had reached Billy and, true to his leather nature, pulled the duct tape off his mouth in one quick motion. Billy was just too scared to scream, but confirmed that Brandy was the bad guy by pointing at him. After calling an ambulance, the police were able to get a short statement from Billy. When the ambulance came, Colin called to Derek and Al to follow them to the hospital. He never figured out how they had managed to make it to Billy's apartment from the bar.

Billy was checked out completely by a tired resident who was bracing for another weekend night in the city. Other than scared out of his wits, he was hung over, and had a huge bruise all around his neck and on his face where Brandy had hit him. The police came and took a formal statement. It seems that Billy had gone to the bar and was drinking rather heavily because he was upset about another fight with his boyfriend in Columbus. Brandy came and sat down beside him. In the process of consoling him, offered to take him home and show him what a real man could do. Once they got to Billy's apartment, Brandy had started off by stripping him and tying him up. After that, it went down hill. Brandy started calling him a filthy faggot and said that the world had enough of his kind. He started hitting Billy, who thought that this was just a very intense S/M scene. When he tried to say that it had gone far enough, Brandy taped his mouth shut and told him that he was about to be rehabilitated, permanently. Then the rope came out and he told Billy that he was about to join the other faggot who played with the priest boy and his lover top. Billy knew that he was talking about Vlad and got very scared. He kept pulling on the rope making it tighter and tighter each time. When Billy started to cry, it only made Brandy meaner. He certainly wanted to kill Billy, but he wanted to see him suffering and scared first. When the police were done, they had enough information to keep Brandy in jail—he confessed to a murder, and was caught in the act of attempting another. They left Billy and Colin in the small emergency department examining room. Of course, they were at the hospital where Colin worked.

With the tired permission of the resident, Colin offered to take Billy home. He would come home with him, Derek, and Al. Billy didn't resist. He didn't want to be alone that night. When they came out of the room, Derek ran over and put his arms around his lover.

"Hey, I wasn't the one who was almost murdered," Colin said trying to lighten the situation a little.

"I just realized how much I love you," Derek answered and then went over to hold Billy in his arms for a few minutes.

Colin and Al went to get the car. They came back quickly and picked up Derek and Billy. That night they went home to Colin's big king size wooden bed. They all took showers and Colin made them some drinks. Billy was very quiet, and a little anxious. Colin had a sedative that the resident had given him, as well as a prescription for them. He gave the pill to Billy, turning the air conditioning up and put him under the blankets. He joined Derek and Al in the living room. For a few minutes, the three men just stared out into space. Finally, Colin broke the silence.

"I'm curious Derek, how did you know that Billy was in danger?"

"Colin, I know that you're confused, let's just say that I can't talk about it."

"But....."

Al interrupted, "Colin, sometimes you just have to trust a priest and drop it at that."

Al had already determined how Derek knew about Brandy when they were in the bar, given the conversations that the two priests had over the last couple of months. He could see the relief in Derek's eyes now that the ordeal was over, and could see the conflict there as well, knowing that the priest was concerned that his silence had almost cost another life.

"Well, I have to hand it to you boys, you certainly know how to have a really fun evening. You got me all horny, then blew it," Colin said with a little smile crossing his face.

"Well, we could still get it on a little bit," his lover offered.

The three men looked as if they were considering the thought, then said, almost in unison, "NO!" It just didn't seem right to start to have some major S/M scene right after a good friend of theirs almost lost his life to one.

"Let's just go to bed," Derek said.

They went upstairs and all climbed into the bed. Al and Derek were on one side while Colin put his arms around Billy and held him tightly. Within a few minutes they joined Billy in his realm of dreams. The next morning they all woke up about the same time, with four men horny as hell. Colin was stilled turned on by the preliminaries from the night before. Derek and Al were still turned on because they had expected a major session. Billy was turned on because he was Billy and he was twenty-three.

Sex that morning was a casual kind of play with Colin fucking Billy and holding him tightly while Derek and Al sucked Billy's cock and played with his nipples. All of the men came quickly and spent the rest of the day in a daze. They didn't really do anything. It was as if they were afraid to leave the house.

Derek got up the next morning and dutifully conducted the liturgy at St. Swithen's. The Rector's spouse was noticeably absent. As a matter of fact, none of the men went to church that morning. After the liturgy, Derek went and got bagels and donuts for the household. He came back to the rectory, made coffee, prepared a tray, and stopping to pick up the paper, took it to the upstairs study.

They were like refugees, gathering around the carafe of coffee that morning. No one was saying too much. Colin finally broke the spell and said, "You know guys, we are going to have to leave this house at some point in time."

"I know," Billy replied, and after a few minutes added, "but it has been great hiding out here. I am totally freaked out by what happened Friday night. You always told me to be careful, I just didn't think anything like that would happen in sleepy little Pittsburgh."

As the men continued to discuss Friday night, Al opened the Sunday paper. There on the front page was a picture of the four of them leaving the hospital on Saturday morning. The caption read: *Ritual S/M Murderer in Pittsburgh.* The article went on to identify Billy as the victim, with his friends who frequent the local leather bar: Colin Morgan, administrator of the hospital, Rev. Derek Wilson, Rector of St. Swithen's Episcopal Church, and Fr. Al D'Amore, a Roman Catholic priest on a leave of absence. He was dumbfounded. There wasn't any pictures of Brandy, the perpetrator, just the four men. Oh, the whole story was retold in the article, including that Brandy was a married man with children who owned a leather bar where men could go to engage in 'ritual S/M practices'. It also touched on the fact that he was awarded Papal Knighthood recently and that he murdered people. When there was a lull in the conversation, he read the article to his friends, showing them their picture.

Colin looked at Derek who had turned white as a ghost. "Well there goes my ecclesiastical career."

"Not to mention that fact that I won't have much credence as the local hospital administrator," added Colin.

"And the fact that I think my decision to leave the Roman Catholic Church has been made for me," added Al.

"This is far out! I will be a celebrity in the bar!" Billy chimed in, not recognizing the his was the only response that had any positive note to it.

"Well, you said that you wanted to leave Pittsburgh, Derek, what do you say that we look for jobs tomorrow, somewhere else?" Colin asked, grabbing his lover's hand.

"I wonder how many people in church this morning read that and didn't say anything to me."

"I wonder how many of my ex-parishioners read that and are counting their children to make sure that I didn't ritually slay any of them," Al replied and the four men started to laugh. It was really the first time that they laughed since the incident.

There was no sense of catastrophe among the men, just a quiet resolve that they must move on. Colin made the point that the parish would probably stand behind Derek on this. And that he could remain at the hospital. It would look bad to get rid of someone because of what they do in their private life, not to mention the human rights issues involved. He did however, make the point that this was probably a good reason to start the process of moving.

Al became a little anxious, not knowing if his new relationship with two men instead of the usual one-on-one was about to come to an end. No one was mentioning him coming   along, or looking for a job. He felt like his whole world was crumbling around him. Maybe he should just forget everything and throw himself on the mercy of his bishop. He pondered the thought of spending the rest of his days in some rural outpost in the far west.....the priest who fell from grace.

That afternoon, Colin called a vice president at the hospital and requested a two week leave with pay. It was granted without comment. The vice-president was, in all probability, relieved that Colin wouldn't be in the office. Hospital administrators shouldn't be dodging reporters while they are on the job. He rejoined his friends and proposed a game plan.

"Derek, when can you check the available clergy positions in the country?" He asked his lover.

"It would be better if I checked tomorrow, but I doubt that anyone will want the BDSM priest bottom."

"Well, we don't know that yet, there might be someplace with a large gay population in the parish. After you do that, I'll make some calls and see where I could get a job in the same locale. . . Al, do you have any restrictions on where you want to live?" Colin asked, turning to the other man.

"I thought that you would never ask! No, I'll go anywhere, but are you guys sure that you want me to tag along?" Al replied.

"You're a part of us now Al," Derek added, "It might be only for a short while or for the long haul, but you are a member of this family."

"Hey guys, what about me?" Billy chimed in.

"Billy, do you really want to be tied down with a bunch of older men?" Colin asked.

"Colin, tying down is not the way I would put that right now."

"My mistake. But don't you want a relationship of your own?" Colin added.

"I don't mean that I want to be like the three of you, or maybe I do, but not on the same level. I need a change of scenery. You guys are hot. It would be fun. I would like a little more freedom than Derek and, I guess, Al, but I wouldn't mind living with you guys for a while. You know that I like to play with you."

"We all know how you like to play with Colin, Billy," Derek replied.

"Do I detect a sense of bitchiness in that, Derek?" Colin asked looking at the man that he thought was his lover, but was not sure what the relationship should be called now.

"Not at all, I was always glad whenever you would stop by Billy's. It made you calmer."

"Amazing! I had no idea that you knew.   Now that we're moving and opening up this relationship to another, I'm not sure of my position. I guess that I will no longer be called the Rectorina. However, I don't know what to call you guys either.....how about Honorable Wife, Honorable Concubine, and Boy?"   Colin added, and then the men began to laugh all over again. He was anxiously awaiting Monday and the beginning of their escape.

Chapter 17

That Monday morning came all too quickly. The parish phone was ringing off the hook. Many of the calls were from the Bishop's office, repeatedly asking to speak to the Rector. Then there were the personal calls on the other phone, friends asking what happened and reporters asking for a story. Colin and Derek had breakfast alone, Billy going back to his apartment and to work, while Al went over to the apartment he rented but rarely spent any time in.

"Where do you want to live, Derek?" Colin asked his lover.

"Where ever we can get jobs."

"Have you looked this morning yet?"

"Well I did. There's a couple way out west in small towns, and a few that are wealthy established churches. I think we can forget both, but for markedly different reasons," Derek answered, looking out the window of the coffee shop that the found themselves in.

"Any other prospects?"

"I don't want to tell you this, but I will. I'm not sure of the city, it really seems boring to me."

"What city is it?" Colin asked, wishing that his lover would just once supply information without a surgical extraction.

"Columbus, Ohio."

"That's great. There's a visible gay community there—vibrant from what I can tell."

"Not to mention, Republicans, white bread people, and your ex-lover," Derek said, turning his head and facing his lover.

"Come on Derek, you know that's over."

"I know, but he's so depressing, I'm sure that the weather would always be damp and gray simply because of his very presence in the city. Besides, I don't know anything about the church, except that it's gay friendly."

"That's a start. Which one is it?"

"St. Peter's, right in the city. But remember, gay friendly doesn't mean give me your tired, your lonely, your HIV positive priest involved in a ritual S/M death scandal in Pittsburgh."

"I've been there. It's great. And I'm sure that they will take you. It's small, and doesn't look particularly rich or established," Colin said, relieved that there seemed to be at least one answer to all of the questions that they had this morning.

"The salary will be low. What will you do? What about Al? Where would we live?"

"I bet that I can get a job in Columbus. It might not be a great job, but I can get one. Remember, we have the money from the sale of my condominium, the money my grandmother gave me, plus the money I have been saving."

"And how much is that, my little dreamer lover?" Derek asked.

"Last time I checked we had about $750,000. Seems like enough to get started somewhere else to me. But let me make a call and see if I can arrange anything there for myself."

"You're kidding!" Derek exclaimed, sitting there with his mouth wide open.

"No, I have some friends, I can see if there's any job available in the hospital."

"No, not that! We.....you have that much money?"

"We have that much money. It's ours. Yes. Your dad has been going over our books each Christmas, didn't he tell you?"

"You know that I don't pay too much attention to money."

"Right, but we have it. So I can take a lower paying job, and with your money, and Al's if he's serious, we can make it. Contact the church."

"Are you OK with this Al thing?" Derek asked.

"Let me start by asking you if you're OK with it."

"Yes, I am. Not sure how it's all going to turn out, but OK, even happy about it. With the three of us, there's less pressure on any two of us. But I'm probably not making myself clear."

"I understand, I think. But there is one thing that I want to remain the same."

"What is that?" Derek asked.

"You and I have a bond, a really strong one, for all of the human frailty that we have brought with us into this thing. I don't want to lose that. I want us to be the central unit, and Al can be as close as any third can be."

"I don't think that it's going to be easy, especially with that requirement."

"Has anything ever been easy for us?"

"Well, we got into the habit of loudly discussing our differences, we did that pretty easily Colin."

"Has it been that bad? Do you want to use this as an excuse to leave me?"

"Not at all, I love you more today than I did when we first met and I didn't think that would be possible. I can't imagine not being with you, talking to you, making love to you, and yes, sometimes arguing with you. Why are leather tops always so insecure?"

"Probably because we always find ourselves with younger men," Colin answered and got up to pay the check. Funny how lovers always know when it's time to leave a restaurant without asking. Two people really do begin to be able to read each other's body language.

That night they all gathered for dinner. After dinner, Colin and Derek talked about the plans they started to make that morning. Derek had called the church and it seemed like they were willing to take him on, even after he told them of his current predicament. They wanted him to come out that week for an interview, to, as he said, make sure that he didn't have two heads or something. Colin had called a friend of his at one of the hospitals there and was assured that there would be a position for him, just FAX his resume over, which he did.

"Are you guys still willing to take me along?" Al asked.

"Of course, I guess that we are telling you this to see if Columbus is OK with you. If it is, we can do it. If not, we can rethink it," Colin said.

"I thought that I would just be ordered to go and do it," Al said, smiling the whole time.

"We're not going to even get into that right now, Al." Colin answered.

"I assume that you will have some canonical things to do to leave the priesthood," Derek asked.

"Why should I bother? Would the Episcopal church not take me without the dispensation?"

"Al, you made a vow. Now you want out. Follow the procedure! Don't leave like a renegade," Colin said.

"But, Colin......" Derek began.

"It's over. He will do what has to be done!" Colin said. Derek and Al knew by the look and the tone of the voice that he wouldn't budge on this one. Billy was totally lost in the whole conversation.

Feeling left out, he finally said in all exasperation, "But what about me?"

The three other men laughed out loud, partly because of Billy's intensity and partly because they all understood that, as far as a twenty-three year old is concerned, it was always all about them.

"Well Billy, do you still want to go with us?" Colin asked.

"Of course, it will be fun. Not to mention, great to get out of Pittsburgh."

"Be careful Billy, the grass is not always greener on the other side," Al said.

"When will we leave?" Billy asked.

"Well Derek, when would we leave?" Colin asked, turning to the man who was now the alpha lover of the pack.

"The people at St. Peter's were anxious, it would probably be soon. I will have to wait for a replacement here though, and what about you Colin, how much notice do you have to give the hospital?"

"Well, I don't really think that you will have to continue on here. I'm sure that the bishop would want you out soon and will probably make some interim arrangement for St. Swithen's. I can be out of the hospital in a month's time, that's no problem." Colin replied.

The men spent another hour or so talking excitingly about their move. Al agreed to move his things into the rectory and pay for all of the moving expenses. They were going to do it right – hire a company of strong men to pack them up and move them. Colin said that he would contact someone in Columbus to handle the relocation as far as living arrangements went. There was an area not far from the church that was being reclaimed, mostly by gay men and yuppies. They could find an old Victorian with enough room for four men and their egos. Billy was excited, and ready to become Colin's total slave. The older man wisely told him that he would be his sexual slave from time to time, but that he needed to find his own lover. Colin knew what Billy wanted, and this much-evolved relationship wouldn't satisfy him over time. Billy needed to be with one man exclusively for a while. But, the move would enable him to branch out on his own, with the comfort and safety of a newly formed family.

Billy agreed to find a job, and since it probably wouldn't be a high paying job, he would also do most of the house work. Al was excited and anxious at the same time, wondering if he would find work in Columbus, and if he would remain a priest, switching to the Episcopal Church.

Later that night, Colin arranged for a party of a different sort, in the dungeon. This time, unbeknownst to the rest of the men, he went down and prepared the room. Surrounding the St. Andrew's cross many candles had been arranged and lighted. There were candles in the shelves and along the floor as well. On the shelf rested three leather collars, with two padlocks. A small grill with red hot coals was sitting in the corner, and an iron brand with the initials, CM, was resting in among the coals.

He went upstairs and dressed in full black leather, appearing in the study and ordering the three men to strip and go down into the dungeon. They all scurried down the steps. Colin took a couple of minutes before going down there himself, adding more than anticipation to the scene. Once they were there, he ordered them to kneel. He pissed on all of them, and then had each one suck his cock. After a while, he ordered Derek to go up to the cross. He had Billy place the restraints on his wrists and ankles, then asked Al to help Billy hold Derek. Derek knew what was coming, they had talked about it many times, with Colin always saying that it was too early in the relationship. Finally, when all of them were in place, Colin secured the leather hood on Derek, and went over to the grill. The tension in the room was tangible. Al and Billy looked, with wide eyed wonder, at Colin as he proceeded to complete what he had set out to do. He picked up the white-hot iron and branded his lover's ass with his initials. Derek let out one scream. Immediately after that, Colin grabbed the crushed ice that he had hidden and placed it over the newly burnt skin.

Derek's hood was taken off and he was taken down off the cross. The two other boys had to support Derek, who was overcome with emotion. Colin had the three men kneel again, and he placed the first collar on Billy. Then he came to Al and secured the second collar, placing a lock on the back. Finally, he came to Derek, and put his collar on him and locked it as well. He leaned over and kissed him on the mouth, saying quietly, "Now you are really all mine." He then ordered the three men upstairs and told them to shower, instructing Al to place some antibiotic spray and ointment on the brand.

While they were upstairs, Colin entered the church through the secret passage way. He knelt down in front of the cross and simply stared at it. It was a long time ago, when he was in the seminary himself, that he felt the same way. Nervous about leaving a place he had come to call home, but relieved that the decision was made. While he knew that most of the Christian world wouldn't understand his prayer, he prayed in thanksgiving for Derek. He knew that he loved this man deeply. No matter what was going on in their lives, no matter how tense the situation could be, Derek, in many ways made Colin happy.

He returned to the house and went to the bedroom where three very respectful men waited for him. He took Derek in his arms and kissed him over and over again. Then, reaching for Al, had him enter their embrace. Finally, he put his arm around Billy and kissed him lightly on the mouth. When the magic of the dungeon scene had passed, Al asked if he could be branded sometime.

Colin was silent for a long time after Al asked. Branding for an old guard leather Master was a significant step in a relationship with another man. It wasn't taken lightly or done with the same abandon that various fraternities and sororities were becoming known for. Colin looked at Al for a long time before he responded.

"Well, in several years, if you're still with us, I might consider it," Colin replied.

Without being asked, Billy said, "That's OK for me, I think I'll pass."

"And if I ordered you to be branded, boy?" Colin asked.

"I would use my safe word," Billy responded, invoking that special word between two men involved in an S/M scene to let the top know that the scene has to end.

All of the men started laughing. It was the laughter of a family, comforting in its timber. How four very different people came together this closely was truly an amazing thing. That night, the four of them slept entwined on the bed, all dreaming quietly of the adventure that was awaiting them. Each of them, excited at the prospect of beginning again in a new place, making new friends, and experiencing new adventures.

Chapter 18

Colin did get a job in Columbus, not quite as high paying, but a decent salary. The people at St. Peter's welcomed Derek with open arms, and Al began the process of asking for a permanent dispensation from his vows from Rome, and accepting ministry in the Episcopal Church. Billy gave his notice at work, deciding to look for a job when he got to Columbus. The three men were busy with the usual petty things that people have to suffer through when making a major move in their lives.

The remaining month in Pittsburgh was spent in preparing for the move. Even though they hired a professional moving company, there were still those little things that had to be packed, and boxed. Each day they did what they could while fulfilling their responsibilities. Tempers flared at times, but only because they were tired, and anticipated the move with the realization that they were starting over.

Most of their free time was spent saying good byes to friends, and working with the gay man that was arranging their relocation. A great house had been found in the very area that Colin mentioned when they started to make plans. It was in great shape, and Colin arranged for some repairs and painting to be done before they moved. It certainly was big enough, a seventeen room Victorian, over a hundred years old.

It was decided that Billy would be sent ahead the week before the other three men left the city. He would go with the movers and help unpack and arrange. His job was to shelve books, unpack clothes and dishes, and make it so that the other three men would just move in. Colin, Derek, and Al packed a suitcase with enough clothes for the week. Billy had Al's car in Columbus, and the three men joked that he was out at the bars every night, picking up a different man. That was ok, with Billy doing all of the hard work of moving, it was going to be like the three of them coming home from a vacation when they finally got there.

Al still had to reconcile himself with the decisions that he had made, and the decisions that had been made for him. He went to see one of his old priest friends and told him of what had happened. The man told him that, while he didn't understand it, Al still had to follow his heart. That's the way it was with so many holy people. They might not understand the morality or the attraction, but they understood that a person had to follow their heart to be happy. Al wondered when the rest of the Christian world would get the message.

Derek had his last meeting with his bishop, who was totally relieved to be getting rid of this priest. At first, Derek was going to let him have it, then, he decided that he would simply stand there and let the old man have his day. Derek knew that the only power anyone held on another person was power that they had been given—given by the person upon whom the power was held. He wouldn't give the man that power. He was simply polite and left the bishop's office.

Colin finished his work up at the hospital and endured the long good bye process that someone has to endure when they have worked somewhere for any length of time. There were the parties and the endless lunches with people that felt they were his best friends, when, in actuality, to Colin, they were only people that he had worked with. Even he had to forgo telling people exactly what he thought of them – funny, he always thought that was what he would do when it was finally over.

They were living in the empty rectory right now – only having to move the one suitcase, and the dirty clothes and laundry that they were collecting. In many ways, stripped of all of their possessions and only having themselves to come home to, was comforting to the three of them. Sure they were happy to be with each other, and they were excited about the formation of this new kind of family, but they were also sad, even Derek, who hated Pittsburgh. There were friends here and memories for all of them. So they walked around like family members do after someone has died.

On the day that they were to leave, Colin said that he would pick them up in the evening. It was only a three-hour drive, and for some reason, which no one could remember, they had to leave at night. Derek and Al were at the rectory and Colin was going around doing some last minute errands. When he was finished, he went up to Squirrel Hill, to his favorite coffee shop. Colin spent a long time, deep in thought over leaving the comfort of a city that he had come to call home—his home, not the one he inherited from his family. In many ways, it represented his freedom as a gay man –the freedom to choose where one would live, and how a person would form a family. He also pondered the way that his relationship with Derek was evolving. He wondered how Al would fit into it. Eventually, he came to the realization that he would do whatever it would take to make Derek happy. After all, Derek came to Pittsburgh to be with him and to make him happy. Would his move be any less or any more expected in the relationship? He marveled at how happy Derek could make him, and how much courage he gained from the realization that he was at his side.

When he was finally rested, and resolved in his decision to leave the city, he got up and paid the bill. It was again August, and the evening breeze was cool, announcing the end of another summer. As he walked to his car, he was strangely happy that he would be moving. Of course, what was not to be happy about—three gorgeous men who would submit to his sexual appetite whenever he wanted it? He was a lucky man. He knew that wasn't the only source of his luck though. He was lucky to have met Derek, and now he was lucky to move some-where where it might be easier for his lover. And he was lucky to have Al with them. He missed Vlad, and he would miss his friends here in Pittsburgh, especially Lee Starr. Colin realized how much he missed Lee, and how much he had loved him, and how much he still loved him. Who knows, perhaps in the future there would be more in the house-hold, all interconnected in some way. Isn't that they way that families, especially leather families came into being? Colin made a mental note to call Lee when the newly formed family was settled in Columbus.

He had one more errand to complete before picking up his lover. He didn't have much time and had to hurry to get it done. He finally pulled up to the rectory and blew the horn. After a couple of minutes, the two other men came out with the suitcase and the dirty laundry. Derek looked at the rectory almost wistfully, experiencing the anxiety that goes along with making a major move. As much as he had hated Pittsburgh, it was home to him for a while, and the first place that he had actually moved in with a lover. It housed many good memories of coming together with a man that he loved. True, there were bad times, and tense times, and times when he didn't think that it could go on any longer, but it did.

Derek wiped a tear from his eye as he walked down the driveway. A tear that was shed as much for his transition from youthful abandon to mature responsibility, as it was for the people that he would miss by moving to Columbus. Al was also quiet and reflective, for he was not only moving away from a place that he had worked, Pittsburgh had been his home as well, and he was leaving his home and his church. As happy as their lives promised to be, this was a moment mixed with emotions. However, for human kind, all of life was mixed with the emotions of happiness and sadness, anticipation and dread.

The two quiet men walked the length of the driveway toward the man awaiting them. They didn't stop to think that he was plagued with just as much anxiety, happiness, anticipation and remorse as they had been. They only knew that each of them, in their own way, loved this man as they loved each other, and that, together, they could face the future. Derek and Al got to the car and threw the laundry and the suitcases in the back. Derek opened the passenger door and was greeted with the comforting smile of his lover and the wet kisses of a six-week-old puppy. As the door closed and Derek nestled the small dog in his arms, he began to cry. The car pulled out with Colin placing his hand on Derek's knee as he looked into Al's eyes in the back seat. The emotion of the moment sealed his resolve to make their lives together work.

The Bonds of Death

Biography

Chuck Williams was born in Pennsylvania in the 1950s. He attended university and several graduate schools, never quite deciding on what he wanted to do with his life. Introduced to leather in the late seventies, he became one of those men dressed completely in black leather, hidden by the shadows in leather bars across the world. While reading and writing are two of his passions, he actu-  ally makes his living in the scientific community. He currently lives in Pittsburgh with his lover, Michael, and a very, very bad dog.

A Boner Book

www.ingramcontent.com/pod-product-compliance
Lightning Source LLC
Chambersburg PA
CBHW071226260626
47162CB00004B/1441